ABOUT THE AUTHOR

Andrew Bullas was born in Worcestershire. After a BA in Fine Art from Portsmouth Polytechnic he attended The London Film School. Subsequently, he has divided his time between independent film-making, teaching and a stint working for the film archive of the Imperial War Museum. He is the founder of Pepwell Productions and an occasional radio show entitled *Plough Your Own Furrow*. *Charlie Echo* is his first book.

CHARLIE ECHO

ANDREW BULLAS

Matador
9 Priory Business Park,
Wistow Road, Kibworth Beauchamp,
Leicestershire. LE8 0RX
Tel: 0116 279 2299
Email: books@troubador.co.uk
Web: www.troubador.co.uk/matador
Twitter: @matadorbooks

'I'm An Old Cowhand (From the Rio Grande)',
Words and Music by Johnny Mercer,

©1936 The Johnny Mercer Foundation (ASCAP),
lyrics reproduced with permission of WC Music Corp

ISBN 978 180046 2267

British Library Cataloguing in Publication Data.
A catalogue record for this book is available from the British Library.

Printed and bound in the UK by TJ Books Limited, Padstow, Cornwall
Typeset in 11pt Minion Pro by Troubador Publishing Ltd, Leicester, UK

Matador is an imprint of Troubador Publishing Ltd

Preface

THE STORY YOU ARE ABOUT TO READ BEGAN after a long sea trip. I had been taking a sabbatical of sorts by crewing on a boat and, just a few days prior to returning to Portsmouth, had decided to adopt a new philosophy. What this boiled down to in practice was simply trying not to worry about things. Or, at least, trying not to worry about them quite as much as I had done before setting sail! The main thing I was going to try not to worry about was looking for a job. However, as I had not earned any money during the time I'd been away and was going to need some pretty urgently, my new philosophy was to be tested almost immediately. I returned home on a Friday in early October and resolved to begin my quest for gainful employment the following Monday. This I duly did by purchasing a copy of the *Guardian* and trawling through its Media Appointments section. As my training and experience were in film-making, I was looking for something that was at least film-related. Although, because of my new Zen outlook, I accepted I might well have to modify my expectations. It was therefore a relief to spot, that very morning, an advertisement for a job in the Film and Video Archive of the Imperial War Museum.

At that time I hadn't really grasped the fact that the IWM was not just the iconic building on Lambeth Road in

London, but also included HMS Belfast, The Cabinet War Rooms, former RAF Duxford and the soon to be opened branch, IWM North. So, in my ignorance, I just assumed the job I was applying for would be based in London and that I, if lucky enough to get an interview, would end up being based there. I was soon to discover that I was mistaken on both counts but, with my new philosophy still firmly in place, I resolved just to go with the flow. And so, it came about that I began working at Duxford and living in nearby Cambridge for the next thirteen years.

For the most part work at the museum revolved around film preservation: the viewing, repairing and preparing of ageing, flammable nitrate negatives prior to their copying onto safety film, thus ensuring their accessibility for future generations. However, sitting alone watching reel after reel of mostly silent black-and-white footage, one couldn't help wondering what the people captured in those moving pictures were thinking or talking about at that particular moment. And then, inevitably, what they might say if they could speak to us in the here and now. True, the museum had within its collection a number of reels entitled *Calling Blighty* in which troops spoke, often awkwardly, to camera and sent messages to loved ones at home, but this footage constituted only a tiny fraction of its holdings. What about all the others who had never had a microphone thrust in front of them? What of their voices?

As mentioned earlier, I had never planned to move to Cambridge. I lived there simply because of its close proximity to Duxford. A case of going where the work was, my new philosophy in action again. As a consequence, it took me a while to start thinking about the city in its own right and what it might have to offer. But when I did, paramount among those attractions was the chance to see a show by the *Cambridge Footlights*, the venerable university comedy troupe that had already assumed legendary status by the time Peter Cook became a member in the early 1960s. I was therefore delighted to get my hands on a ticket for *The Silliad*, that year's Footlights pantomime.

With a couple of glowing exceptions, including a very early production penned by David Wood, I must confess to never having been overly fond of Christmas shows as a child. Don't get me wrong, going to the theatre was always a treat, but these visits to matinees in half-empty auditoriums during that horribly flat period between Christmas and the return to school only served to reinforce the negative impression. However, as the pantomime was the next big show by the Footlights and as I wanted to see them, it was a case of *que sera, sera*. And, guess what? I was completely bowled over by it!

What I realise now is that I'd lucked out in every way. It was Saturday night, it was the last night of the run before the Christmas holidays, the place was packed with family and friends of people involved with the production and the piece itself flew. In fact, prior to the curtain going up, there was such a buzz in the ADC theatre that I had a horrible feeling I'd somehow gatecrashed a private performance and would be asked to leave! Anyway, I stayed put and, within minutes of the curtain rising, knew that this was a show that wanted to embrace its audience warmly and that any notes of division, provocation or exclusion were banished for the duration. What the wonderful cast and gifted writers, who I learned from the programme were Tom Basden, Lloyd

Woolf and Stefan Golaszewski,[1] did so splendidly was use the conventions of pantomime to bring Venus, Bacchus, Plato and a stroppy centaur called Horsio alive in a way that no one could resist. The gulf between the old music-hall style of comedy that had thrived for so much of the twentieth century and its modern, twenty-first-century alternative was bridged. Past and present spoke to each other and the seeds of an idea were planted in my mind.

As to the soundness (all puns intended) of that idea, the reader will have to judge for themselves. But, as I write this on the 75th anniversary of V.E. Day, the world is caught up in yet another battle, this time against a virus. Then as now, discussions are starting to take place about the kind of world people want to live in after things get back to normal and indeed whether the very idea of normal itself needs to change! Time has telescoped and voices that seemed to have belonged to a bygone era are suddenly newly relevant again. These are not the voices of Greek gods but of ordinary men and women, people who muddled through as best they could and knew the value of a joke when they heard one. As a philosophy it may not have been very profound but it worked. It also reminds me of the advice offered by Jack London to aspiring writers: "It does not hurt how wrong your philosophy of life may be so long as you have one, and have it well."[2]

Andrew Bullas
8th May 2020

---

1   Each, unsurprisingly, has gone on to a successful career on stage, screen and radio.
2   Kershaw, Alex, *Jack London – A Life*, London, Harper Collins, 1997, p.87.

Chapter One

A LTHOUGH CHARLIE GOODMAN'S WORKSHOP did look a lot like an Aladdin's cave, few would have cast the man himself in the role of pantomime hero. In fact, on the day this story begins, you'd have been hard pressed to meet anyone less eager to strut their stuff before the footlights. The only light he sought was the one that shone from the angle poise lamp above his bench. But even the least theatrical people can create their own stages, and the dials of the various radio sets which lined the shelves glowed like jewels. And if the buzzing circuit valves did not shine quite like gold, they were at least amber bright and brought the treasure troves of fairy tale and fable to mind. Also, like all caves in such stories, this one was well hidden, not in an Arabian desert, or many days' walk from a Persian oasis, but under the stairs of an electrical shop in Leeds.

And if they could have seen Charlie himself, what would local folk have made of him? The fact that he was pale wouldn't have surprised them. After all, who wouldn't be pale working in a room with no windows or daylight? Thin, too. Well, what of that? Most people were. The war was just over and there was no sign of food rationing ending anytime soon. But they may have thought him a bit young to be a recluse; after all he couldn't be more than late thirties at most. And why, they would've asked in their direct way, was he playing with that alphabet abacus when there was a small child at his feet playing with a dangerous-looking screwdriver? "That's a bit topsy-turvy, isn't it?" To which I would've had to reply, "You're right, it is." But then, that's the way Charlie was at the start of this story. It's also the way a lot of homecoming soldiers were after active service, but we'll get to that.

But, because this is a story about a man who became an echo, it should really begin with a sound and this one began with a shop bell. They're not so common now but back when this story is set, people would place a bell over the door to let them know when a customer entered or left the premises. For Charlie, this bell reminded him of the world outside his cave and, because of that, it made him jump. He jumped then. Without taking his eyes off the abacus he called out in a soft Yorkshire accent, "Shop, Margie." Getting no response, he called again, with a definite trace of anxiety this time, "Margie?"

He was answered by hurried footsteps and seconds later Marge herself appeared. This was Charlie's sister and, although she was perhaps a year or so older, the facial similarities were obvious for everyone to see. But, of course, everyone couldn't see because Marge was also his carer, and the sole public face of the business.

Dragging another small child behind her, she swooped

down, removed the screwdriver from the toddler's grip, substituted it with the abacus and planted the screwdriver back in Charlie's hand.

"I can't be everywhere at once, can I?" she muttered.

Charlie responded by using the screwdriver to point to the abacus and observe, "It might have begun with a D." At which point a less patient woman might have demanded to know what on earth he was on about. But, although Marge could bark, she knew when not to bite. She understood that her brother's head was somewhere else and she, perhaps unusually among siblings, genuinely loved him. So she shook her head and towed the children away to deal with the customer in the shop beyond. Left to his own thoughts again Charlie began to scribble the letter D in a notebook. The pages of the notebook showed the name Charles written over and over again with a variety of second names attached to it: Charles Aired, Charles Baird, Charles Caird, Charles D…

The shop itself was a cheerier place altogether and, aside from the bell and the modest stock of electrical goods that one might expect to find in 1945, not so very different from the small, family-run shops of today. Large windows faced onto the street making the most of the fading December daylight and the mood was lifted further by swags of Christmas paper chains draped from the ceiling. Responding to the positive change of atmosphere, the older child broke free from his mother's grasp and began wandering around the shelves.

Marge glanced from the small boy to the customer and back again. "Now Albert, don't go getting your mucky fingerprints over everything because Detective Inspector

Saunders here will be able to identify them and he'll send you up before the judge." But Albert was no fool. He had seen the man with the shiny shoes and the raincoat come into the shop several times. On each occasion the stranger had only seemed interested in talking quietly to his mother and didn't seem frightening at all.

As soon as the child was out of earshot Saunders drew closer to the counter and nodded in the direction of the strip curtain. "How is he today?"

"Back on the Ds again," sighed Marge.

Then, having caught sight of Albert planting a chubby hand on the poster taped to the front door, she reverted back to her usual brassy self.

"And *don't touch* includes that poster as well."

The child concentrated hard on breaking the bright letters down into syllables.

"A-lad-din".

"Yes, love, that's right, but we saw *Aladdin* year before last, didn't we?"

Albert persisted though. He wasn't done yet. "Uncle Charlie took us."

Marge was caught off guard, but she managed to hold it together.

"He did that. But leave it alone now, there's a good lad."

Finally, the child did as he was told and mooched over to something else.

"The children can't understand why he practically ignores them now. None of us can understand really; how could we?" She paused before bringing her eyes back to Saunders. "Unless we were there, I mean."

The man bent down and lifted a large green canvas case up onto the counter. "That's why I tracked down one of these. It's a W.S. 18, made by Pye. Exactly the same model as we were using in France."[1]

Marge eyed both the man and the case warily.

"Weighs a fair bit, too, by the look of it."

He forced a smile. "Nowhere near as much as a troubled conscience."

Taking hold of the military radio she began to grasp the full implications of his words.

"Nobody's expecting as good as new, but a serviceable repair would be a definite improvement," he continued carefully.

Marge nodded before raising her voice theatrically. "Well, sir, our normal turnaround is two days, but for a complicated job like this it might be a bit longer."

Charlie was writing the name *Charles Dared* in his notebook when he heard, rather than saw, Marge return to the workshop. "What was it?"

"Radio repair," she replied non-committally before releasing the shoulder strap.

"Columbia? Marconiphone? Murphy?"

She didn't reply.

Funny how some names still tripped off the tongue, he thought, *but when you really wanted to remember one in particular, it wouldn't.*

---

1   Pye Ltd was a British electronics company founded in Cambridge, England in 1896. It went on to design and manufacture radio equipment for the British Army. Wireless Set No.18 was the standard British Army Battalion and Company man-pack radio set of WW2. It was used in North Africa, Italy, S.E. Asia, Normandy, Arnhem and the Rhine Crossing. More than 76,000 such sets were produced by Pye and its subcontractors.

Realising she still hadn't answered, he turned around, his eyes settling first on his sister and then on the army radio telephone at her feet.

"It's a Pye, apparently," she said at last.

The dreadful change overtook him before the words had even left her mouth. Although, unbeknownst to Charlie, she'd witnessed such episodes before, they never ceased to disturb her. Often, he would disguise an attack of the shakes by clenching his fists and thrusting them deep into his pockets. As he did so, the sound of the pencil snapping in his palm was unnaturally loud in the small space. It reminded her of a tree she had once seen being struck by lightning. All the electricity in the atmosphere had conspired to wound the one unfortunate thing in its path, and she had felt for it.

1944

The W.S. 18 army radio telephone sat on a table outside a French country inn. Charlie stepped back from it in shock, letting the receiver fall and removing his headphones as he did so. His breathing accelerated and he began to shake. Noticing the tremor in his hands he plunged them deep into the trouser pockets of his army uniform.

*

Marge watched as Charlie bent down to pick up the pieces of broken pencil from the floor. As he turned, his elbow caught a pot of screws, sending them hailing down on top of him. He scrabbled around on his hands and knees for a moment before accepting that his trembling fingers were no match for the task. So, he froze just as he was, down on all fours and cowering like a frightened animal. A second passed, then several more, during which his breathing became slower and deeper until, eventually, he felt able to look up at his sister.

"I thought we'd agreed, Margie, domestic appliances only, remember?"

Marge crouched down to his level and very slowly and deliberately began to pick up what he'd been unable to himself. "I know we did, love, but the gentleman that brought it in, well, he seemed to think you knew about such things and, what with the customer always being right, I could hardly argue, could I?"

Even with his nerves jangling, Charlie knew she wasn't telling him everything, but he was too drained to fathom it out just then. It was as much as he could do to force his gaze over towards the radio, up onto Albert's anxious face and then back to his sister again.

"Come on, just for your big sister Margie," she persisted, "promise me you'll give it a go, eh?"

Chapter Two

ALTHOUGH SHE HAD EVERY RIGHT TO WEAR the uniform of a Land Girl,[2] the outfit might have been designed for Fiona personally, so well did it suit her energetic and purposeful character.

As it was, on this particular evening, the wide-brimmed hat, green wool sweater and brown corduroy trousers had been supplemented by a heavy old coat which kept out the cold while she locked up the hen house. Once the latch had been bolted, she picked up a basket of eggs and made her way towards a castle silhouetted against the darkening sky.

The pile was Victorian Gothic, not as vast as some places but one only had to see the kitchen to grasp its scale. Of the two doors beside the chimney, one led to a pantry whilst the other provided access to the kitchen garden and assorted outbuildings. It was through this that Fiona now

---

2   Originally instituted as a volunteer army during the First World War, the Women's Land Army started conscripting women into work from December 1941 when the National Service Act was passed. Many of the girls came from cities to live and work on the land and by 1943 there were 80,000 workers registered.

entered, passing close by a man tending a saucepan on the stove. The man was Angus, just the kind of robust, no-nonsense character you'd want to call on in a crisis, or any other time for that matter. Impressed by the contents of her basket, he turned to the two young children standing beside him. "Looks like it's boiled eggs for tea, children."

The girl smiled but the boy didn't share her enthusiasm.

"I'm tired of eggs."

"You don't know when you're well off, son. Your sister Martha here's old enough to remember when we didnae see a fresh egg from one month to the next. Just egg powder, and not too much of that either." He caught Fiona's eye and grinned. Suitably chastised, the boy, whose name was Cameron, fell silent.

"Will we really have to go back to Glasgow, Dad?" asked the girl.

The man stopped stirring and, although he addressed his answer to the children, he used his spoon to gesture to Fiona.

"Well, that's not down to me, sweetheart, it's down to the man in the cellar."

"Boo to the cellar man," Martha replied with feeling.

"Hush up, my weans, or he'll hear ye! Now go help synd the rest of those eggs."

As they took Fiona's place at the sink, the two adults tiptoed over to a doorway that led to the cellar and listened.

"How long's he been down there?" the Land Girl asked, adopting a stage whisper.

"At least an hour," answered the chef, also in hushed tones. "Fergus got a lot of the malts out this morning but nearly all the vino is still in the racks."

"Damn," was all she managed by way of reply.

Approaching footsteps put paid to any further discussion and, by the time a slightly breathless and annoyed-looking man appeared in the doorway, both chef and the Land Girl were back at their respective workstations.

The figure now surveying them was of medium height, brooding countenance and carried a clipboard. Had he been played by an actor of the period, James Mason would have done him proud.[3] The only qualifier being that James Mason was born a Yorkshireman, like our hero, and so, even when cast as the villain, was never entirely unlikeable. This was Ivan; as to whether he was truly terrible with it, the reader must decide for themselves.

"Ah Fiona," he began, "perhaps you can explain how two dozen bottles of claret seem to have vanished since I checked last?"

The Land Girl took a second to gather herself before turning around.

"I expect they have been brought up ready for tomorrow. Castle Caird has always prided itself on offering fine hospitality. Would you have it that we should change now?"

Striding over to the middle of the room he leant on the table with clenched knuckles.

"I'd have it that we were a little more discerning. After all, it's a valuable asset."

---

3   James Mason, 1909–1984, was an English actor born in Huddersfield, Yorkshire. At the time of our tale he had become particularly famous for playing screen villains in such British productions as *The Wicked Lady* and *The Seventh Seal*. He later went on to have a highly successful career internationally.

"Aye well, so are its people," she shot back. "And if the first Hogmanay of peacetime isn't occasion enough for uncorking a few good bottles, then I don't know what is."

She had just resumed egg-wiping duty when another man entered by way of a swing door and trotted down some steps. His jaunty demeanour was seriously at odds with the atmosphere of the room, a fact that he picked up on at once, but which did nothing to deter him from his purpose.

"Don't mind me," he announced breezily, "just getting a bottle of her Ladyship's special for supper."

Angus shook his head and growled as the new arrival continued straight towards the cellar door. "You're timing's so off, pal."

He was right, of course, and on more than one count, for not only was it an unfortunate moment to be running such an errand, but also the genial man was indeed his pal, even if he was also a trial. It was a situation experienced by many who went through life being one half of a set of twins. Even so, the fact remained that Angus, being all of five minutes older, was never shy of exercising the prerogative of big brothers everywhere in pointing out the shortcomings of his younger sibling. Their parents, for their part, had managed the tricky task of acknowledging the respective differences and genetic similarities of their two boys by naming them Angus and Fergus.

Ivan dealt with the issue by ignoring Fergus entirely and addressing Fiona instead.

"Can't he tell her to make do with what's out already?"

"No, he can't," she snapped back as the colour rose in her cheeks. "It's about the only pleasure left to her these days."

If he'd not been so easy-going Fergus might've been miffed by Ivan's treatment; instead he just asked evenly, "Have you not seen the way her eyes light up this time of an evening? Fairly sparkle, they do, just like they did before…"

But the man with the clipboard cut him short, "If Fergus knows what's good for him, I think he'll do as I suggest."

Sighing, Fergus turned to Fiona, "Miss?"

With great reluctance Fiona indicated that Fergus should move away from the cellar door and only then did Fergus's temper show signs of flaring.

"I'll do what *you* say, miss, whether or no."

In other circumstances, she would have positively glowed at such loyalty from a colleague. Building a team had been a particular goal of hers ever since coming to work for the estate, and although she had always been willing to roll up her sleeves and get stuck in, the fact that characters like the twins should defer to her judgment was a victory indeed, but one made bittersweet by its timing.

"I'm sure no one should risk losing their job on my account," she murmured before hurrying away and hoping her emotions didn't betray her.

Continuing on through the swing door she crossed the hallway towards the foot of the staircase to the main house. The staircase, which was as wide and deep as you might expect, had a crimson carpet running all the way down and, sailing centre stream, was a dignified craft, otherwise known as Lady Caird.

"Do you know what the most extraordinary thing about Ivan is?" Fiona asked just as the older woman reached the bottom step.

"No, but I have a feeling you're about to tell me," sighed Lady Caird.

"Of all the assets he's so assiduously noting, he's completely incapable of taking people's feelings into account."

It was at moments like this that Lady Caird felt her age. When she was the same age as the girl standing before her, she might have felt the same, but that was a long time ago.

"The Laird can do what he likes, you know that," she replied tiredly.

"But he's not the bloody Laird yet, is he?" fumed Fiona.

"A mere formality, I think," Lady Caird continued carefully. "In fact, I have a feeling that…"

She was startled by the shouts of two scruffy boys, of about eight or nine years old, who had just started sliding down the bannisters, one after the other. They narrowly missed her as they whooshed past, jumped off at the bottom and disappeared down a corridor. Seconds later a small, breathless woman appeared trotting down the stairs in pursuit. This was Amy, the housekeeper.

"I'm so sorry, Lady Caird," she gasped. "I'm trying to get them into the bath and they're not for going." Then she was gone, too, her voice fading away down the corridor. "Donald and Patrick McPherson, you are both wicked wee bairns and when I get my hands on you…"

"Sticks and stones may break my bones, but words will never hurt me," the two boys chanted back cheekily.

"Out of the mouths of babes," Lady Caird smiled wistfully to Fiona before resuming her stately progress.

Fiona tried to smile back but her face muscles refused to co-operate. All she could do was nod her head and run up the stairs as quickly as possible.

Now, you might have expected someone like Lady Caird to have taken great exception to being interrupted by two tykes sliding down her bannister and generally running amok. However, as noted before, many things were topsy-turvy at the time our story takes place. And if she seems more accepting of circumstances than Fiona, it was not just because she was older, but because she had learned to keep many of her true feelings hidden.

Fiona, at this point, was finding it impossible to do the same. Bursting into a room that led off another corridor at the top of the stairs, she slammed the door behind her and leant against it. Although her refuge was still referred to as the library, it also doubled as a sitting room and an office. The days of being able to heat three separate rooms for three different purposes had ended back in 1939.

Nevertheless, with its books and furnishings it made a much more homely impression than the cavernous kitchen on the floor below. She glanced up at the painting above the fireplace from which a soldier in army uniform smiled back at her, only she was in no mood to be mollified just yet. "Oh yes, you can grin, soldier boy, but let me tell you this, sometimes the words left unspoken cause just as much pain as the ones that are." Suddenly a tear ran down her cheek and she brushed it away crossly before moving over to the hearth.

"God knows I've tried to carry out your wishes, or what I imagined your wishes to be, but with no formal pointers…"

Tossing a log into the grate, she wiped away another tear as the flames began to catch and the wood to crackle.

"Come on, Charles. If this old log can answer me back why the hell can't you?"

There was no reply of course, and she didn't really expect one, but just like the fire, she was blazing.

"*Charles?* I'm still waiting for an explanation, damn it!" Then, ending the outburst with a bang rather than a whimper, she threw the poker against the stonework and flopped into a chair. Gradually her breathing slowed, the eyes grew heavy and a clocked chimed far away.

Chapter Three

S OMEWHERE A CLOCK STRUCK TWELVE. CHARLIE'S lips were dry, and he licked them. Then, grabbing a screwdriver, he began to loosen the rear panel of the army radio telephone, muttering to himself as he did so.

"It's a right old riddle, that's what it is. A man with only half a name and a name with only half a man. In but one respect are they the same, solve it if you can."

The panel came free and he placed it carefully to one side before peering into the case. "And solve it you will, my lad. You must."

Suddenly, an authoritative voice answered back, "It's Caird!"

Charlie peered deeper into the case before fearfully glancing round at the doorway, "What the…"

1944

A man in khaki uniform, his face deep in shadow, lay twitching in the dirt.

*

It's a strange thing how we often get what we want but not in the form we want it, and this is what happened to Charlie then. The conventions of pantomime would have us believe in spells and magic, but Charlie had grown out of such things long before he outgrew short trousers. On the other hand, as a former army radio operator, he understood that words had power, often spelling out the difference between life and death. The fact that he had turned the problem that was preoccupying him into a rhyme was something he had done subconsciously. But a rhyme is often about connecting different things in new and surprising ways.

And where some might have used the technique to serve the broad humour of the music halls, others found deeper truths. The ancients might have even recognised it as a form of incantation.

Charlie froze as the khaki-clad figure crawled to his feet and stumbled into the room. At closer quarters he appeared to be around forty and of quite stocky build.

"My name, is Charles Caird," he announced matter-of-factly before brushing the dust from his uniform. Noticing several bullet holes in the tunic, he then placed a hand over them before pulling it away again. Although there were bloodstains on the material, his hand remained clean.

Charlie recoiled at the sight.

"Charles Caird!" he gasped.

"So you can see me too?" the new arrival continued

evenly. "That old ectoplasm stuff must really work after all."[4]

"Flippin' 'eck-toplasm!" Charlie gasped again, for he was prone to a bad pun just as much as a rhyme.

For some, the fact that there are now two characters called Charles may seem unnecessarily confusing. However, although both men may have had the same first name on their birth certificates, Charles's family and friends would never have condescended to call him Charlie, nor would he have allowed them to do so. Charlie, on the other hand, had never been referred to as Charles. He had always seemed too genial and approachable for such formalities, or at least he had done until the war took its toll. Charles, meanwhile, though he would have described himself as a *hale fellow, well met*, also embodied the slightly overbearing manner of someone who felt he was born to lead. This meant he had been well suited to the life of an officer in the British army but, now that that period of his life was over, his whole life in fact now being over, he was not so well equipped for establishing easy rapport with someone from a different background. These two men were two sides of the same coin but, anyone thinking of calling the toss would have been missing the

---

4   "It is curious to observe in a whole gallery of Victorian and Edwardian worthies almost a double life. There is a surface image of the bluff and hearty clubman and public servant, the pipe smoke and the tweeds, the bracing early morning walks and the rigours of the full English breakfast. But behind this there is a powerful inner spirit – beliefs in reincarnation and communication across the void, the desire to peer through "the gap in the curtain" to make contact with "the people of the mist". It is no coincidence that it should revive so powerfully in wartime, when nation and Empire were as one, when the old imperialist Winston Churchill was at the helm and death was all around." Aldgate, Anthony and Richards, Jeffrey, *Britain Can Take It*, Edinburgh University Press, 1994, p. 54.

point. They were both *heads* and they were both *tails*, but to make matters simpler we shall now refer to Charles by his surname.

Although the apparition terrified Charlie it also held him transfixed. Afraid to look and yet afraid to look away in case the phenomenon should disappear again, his hand scrabbled around for a pencil. That found, he scrawled the name in his notebook before repeating it quietly.

"Caird, Caird."

"No hyphen and no double barrel," corrected the visitor.

"I never thought there was," stammered Charlie, "... more than one syllable, I mean. But I went through all the possibilities with just one, over and over. I even thought it was *Baird* sometimes." He paused and looked at the stranger again. "You know, like the inventor of television?"

"You technical blokes," Caird snorted before starting to pace around the room. "Proper Aladdin's cave this workshop, isn't it? All you need do is substitute that radio there for a lamp and the genie for a..." he paused and, before he knew he'd even done it, Charlie finished the sentence for him.

"Ghost!" he gulped.

"And there you have it," smiled Caird as he glanced back at the radio repairman. "Funny thing is, I always thought that manifestation business you heard mediums going on about was all guff, but apparently not. Bloody smoky though, isn't it?" He paused to sniff the air.

Despite his racing brain, Charlie sniffed too. "Burnt sprouts," he managed to reply.

The ghost poked his head out into the doorway and found the smell even stronger outside.

"Then again, it could be your tea spoiling. I'd check the stove if I were you."

Charlie sat staring at the man's uniform and the officer stripes on his arm; the ghost followed his gaze. "Go on, man. There's no point in standing on ceremony. I'm assuming these officer stripes are pretty immaterial now, just like the rest of me."[5]

As Charlie made his way through a cloud of smoke, Caird leant against the door frame and watched the scene unfold with some amusement. The smoke was most definitely coming from the stove and from one saucepan in particular. Charlie lifted the plate off the top to peer inside and burnt himself in the process. Letting the plate fall to the floor with a smash, he grabbed a tea towel and threw the smouldering pan into the sink.

"Bugger," he spluttered before remembering he had an audience and elaborating for their benefit,

"I hate to see good food go to waste."

"Me too," replied the ghost with feeling.

What made Charlie even more despondent was the fact that this little routine was a regular occurrence. Marge would prepare a meal for him and leave it on the stove to heat before returning to her own home each evening. She would remind Charlie about it before she left and he would promise to remember, but he hardly ever did. This frustrating cycle was just one of the many

---

5   Within several days of the Normandy landings, officers had learned to wear their pips on their sleeves instead of conspicuously on their shoulders, thus making them slightly less easy prey for snipers. Baron, Alexander, *From the City, From the Plough*, IWM, 2019, p.137.

things that troubled him about his life, but normally he could cover the traces, or so he thought. But now, because someone else was there to see, he felt that he must try to explain.

"My mind… it slips a cog sometimes," he confessed with embarrassment.

"I know, that's why I've been looking for you," the ghost replied before confusing matters considerably by allowing his eyes to settle on an object resting in a corner. "Broom?"

"Who?" asked Charlie, mightily alarmed at the prospect of a second ghostly arrival.

"I meant you'll need a broom – for that broken plate there," sighed the ghost as he indicated the dustpan and brush nearby.

"Oh, aye," Charlie exclaimed with huge relief.

As the radio repairman began sweeping, Caird returned to the purpose of his mission.

"I couldn't rest without getting everything tied up, you see."

"Get what tied up?"

"My will, damn it."

"You should always write things down," Charlie soothed as he picked up the pan and emptied its contents into the rubbish bin.

"It was a verbal will."

"I have to write everything down otherwise…"

"*But you did write everything down!*" the ghost exploded. "And what's more, you and that other bloke promised to deliver it!"

Anxiety clouded the radio repairman's face yet again as he tried to piece the meaning of Caird's words together.

"I promised?" he asked slowly, as the wheels of his mind began to whirr and grind. Come to think of it, he did have a recollection of making a promise to someone to do something and, whatever it was, it was waiting for him, quite near, very near. Then he had it. "Yes, that's right. I did, didn't I? I promised Margie!"

With that he stumbled away leaving the ghost no alternative but to follow.

Happily settled on his stool once more, Charlie flicked a switch on the army radio telephone. With so many things to press and dials to turn a wag might have renamed him Buttons, but Buttons belongs in *Cinderella*, which is a different pantomime altogether... then again, maybe it isn't. As we've seen already, during the war and its aftermath, people from vastly different worlds found themselves all mixed together in one overarching narrative. Be that as it may, the radio still didn't work and Caird began to pace as he tried to think of the best way to handle the situation.

Suddenly, one of the dials on the set lit up and when the needle began to jerk in response to a piercing shriek of static, both Charlie and the ghost jerked too. Charlie, in particular, seemed mesmerised by the arc of the needle's swing, and all the while a hum coming from the set grew louder. Soon the hum had grown into a drone, a siren song that had him reaching for his notebook.

"I wrote down everything," he murmured as if in a trance. "Everything except your second name and your address because something happened and I couldn't write anymore."

Even Caird was notably subdued when he asked, "But

what about my identity tags, surely they would've helped you trace me?"

Charlie shook his head slowly, "No, I… we… there just didn't seem to be any more of you… anymore!"

Chapter Four

A "CLAY" FLEW INTO THE AIR ONLY TO BE shattered by a loud gunshot. There were assorted cheers as the fragments fell to earth leaving wisps of cordite drifting in the winter breeze. Then, in the following pause, several children, including Cameron and the scruffy boys, burst through the party of adults to retrieve the largest bits of debris from the grass. Amy took advantage of the lull to weave amongst the guests urging them to take another glass from her tray. Elsewhere, the ever-reliable Angus was busy reloading the trap for the next batch of clays and Fiona was chatting to a distinguished, grey-haired man in his seventies.

"Having fun, Finlay?" she asked.

"I always do at your end-of-year bashes," he twinkled back. "Even more so since you and Charles had the idea of having the guns and the beaters all enjoying their sport together. It's so much more inclusive than in the old days."

"Make the most of it then, for if Ivan has his way the old days will be making a comeback."

The old man's face fell, "No olive branches in the offing?"

"Not even a twig. There's no way he's going to wait seven years. It's taken all my female cunning just to stall him this long."

"All set, sir," Angus called. "We're almost out of clays, so you best test your aim now."

The old man nodded whilst Fiona squeezed his arm and left him to try his luck. Finlay raised his gun, Angus released the mechanism, and another clay was obliterated.

Over by a trestle table Fergus was serving hot toddies. As Fiona was passing he caught her eye and indicated that the tureen he was using was nearly empty. No sooner had he left to get a refill than Ivan appeared.

"Still intent on playing the Lady Bountiful?"

"Just trying to do the right thing in the circumstances."

"In the circumstances I wonder you feel you have any right at all. In fact..."

But before he could say more, Lady Caird floated by with the kind of timing that one suspects is entirely deliberate but can't be proved to be so.

"Ivan," she called lightly.

"Aunt Morag?"

"About this evening," she continued, steering him a little distance away. "I was wondering if you'd help me greet the guests? I do so miss having a man around on social occasions like these and it would be a chance for you to meet your future tenants."

Before Ivan could answer, Fiona called after them, "You can serve them with their eviction notices at the same time if you like. It'll save on postage stamps!"

Lady Caird gave a backwards glance, "Fiona!" she tutted, but although the voice was regal there was the trace of a smile on her lips.

"Just being economical," the Land Girl called back before walking briskly towards the castle.

*

"Will you hurry up?" Caird snapped.

What had seemed like a breakthrough when the repairman began working on the set the previous night now seemed like a false dawn. All the more frustrating because now it really was dawn, and all this radio chappie seemed to have done in the interim was fiddle around with a screwdriver and a soldering iron. Caird had actually slipped away in the wee small hours to stretch out on the shop counter.

"Well, so much for the saying 'You can sleep when you're dead,'" he reflected bitterly.

It was just another bit of tosh spoken by the living about a subject they had no understanding of. There was just too much on his mind for any shut-eye and so, when he'd finally heard the radio crackle and pop again a few moments before, he'd attempted to press his case for a second time. But as to how much the Yorkshireman had managed to grasp, he remained frustratingly unsure.

"I need my pencil," came a voice from the workshop.

Caird slid off the counter again and poked his head through the strip curtain.

"I only had it a minute ago," continued Charlie. As he rummaged around the workbench, he noticed a note pinned to a shelf, exactly at eye height. "DON'T LET YOUR TEA BURN DRY!" it said. The repairman snatched it down and screwed it up in frustration.

"It's there!" the ghost said pointing.

"Where?"

Thinking the ghost was pointing to the chest pocket of his brown work coat Charlie reached in and pulled out a screwdriver.

"No, on the bench beside you!" sighed the ghost.

At last Charlie found what he was looking for and was ready to venture into the shop.

The overhead lights came on first, followed by the dials of all the radios. Then, as if on cue, a cat appeared and draped itself over a set positioned on a high shelf. This little ritual complete, Charlie moved over to the telephone, which was screwed to the wall behind the counter. Flicking through his notepad he located the previous night's entry to which had now been added a Scottish-sounding place name and a three-digit number.

Propping the book open with one hand, he lifted the receiver with the other so Caird could start dialling. But just as he handed it over it fell straight through the ghost's grasp. For a moment they both watched dumbly as the apparatus writhed and twisted at the end of its flex, then the ghost fixed Charlie with a stare that brokered no argument.

Despite his apprehension, the operator's voice, when she answered, proved surprisingly reassuring to the repairman's ears. Precise and matter-of-fact, she could have been requesting the name and serial number for a valve or some other technical bit of kit. Nothing more was needed and nothing more was given. There was a minimal margin for error or confusion, just like a wiring diagram. But with a wiring diagram, if he got it right, the problem was solved. If he got this right, things would only get more complicated. Evidently, he had got this bit right for the phone quickly started ringing out at the other end. Resigned to his fate, Charlie moved the receiver to a position where the ghost could hear it too.

Fergus was just passing as the phone rang from its place in the stone passageway.

"Castle Caird?" he answered in his best footman's voice.

"That sounded like Fergus," the ghost announced.

"Hello?" Fergus tried again.

"It *is* Fergus," the ghost beamed.

Still hearing nothing his end, Fergus had begun to frown. Maybe it was just a wrong number but, if it was, surely the caller could at least say so.

"Hello," he tried again.

"Fergus, it's Charles."

Fergus was beginning to lose his patience. Maybe it was those two scruffy nephews of his. This was just the sort of prank they'd try to pull when they knew he was rushed off his feet. But then again, there was no way they'd be holed up in the house when there were guns and excitement outside. So, if not them, who?

"Hello," he tried again, "please state your name and business?"

"Come on, Fergus, it's Charles Caird. Don't tell me you've developed cloth ears while I've been away."

Fergus decided to try one last time. After all, it might

be one of her Ladyship's dotty friends and he'd be sure to get it in the neck if he cut the old biddy off.

"Hello!"

At the other end, realisation finally dawned on the ghost and it was a bitter blow. He had never liked being ignored in life but being ignored in death felt far worse.

"You're the only one who seems to be able to hear me," he murmured to Charlie. "You'll have to speak on my behalf."

Charlie looked from the ghost back to the receiver. This was the last thing he wanted to do but, with the ghost's eyes suddenly looking as desperate as he guessed his own must be, he drew the receiver back to within speaking distance, but still far enough away for Caird to hear both sides of the conversation.

*

Angus glanced at a pile of china being stacked onto a trestle table nearby.

"If you're sure, Miss Fiona?"

"It'll do the job, won't it? she asked briskly. "Besides, I have a feeling we're going to need every ounce of ingenuity from here on in."

The chef acknowledged her point; after all, a saucer was just like a clay in a way. They were both made of the same stuff and as long as the diameter was the same, they should fit into the firing mechanism. In fact, he knew they would fit because he had just made the necessary adjustments. It all boiled down to having the ability to improvise and then being confident enough to back your hunches, and they'd all had to do a lot of that at the castle. But he was aware that outside eyes were now upon them and that they might view such spontaneous invention rather differently. The Land Girl ploughed on regardless, however.

"Roll up, roll up. Step right this way," she cried, and several of the guests did.

During the ensuing barrage of gunfire and shattering china, Fergus emerged from the castle and made his way across the lawn. He carried a large silver salver with an electrical cord dangling from it.

"Call for you, miss," he announced with a grin. He then lifted the lid of the salver to reveal a telephone inside with the receiver off the hook.

"Hello?" she enquired, adopting a playful tone that matched the footman's.

At the other end of the line, just over 200 miles south, Charlie's anxious voice managed to croak "Hello" back.

It wasn't much to go on, but it convinced her that playtime was over.

"Who I am speaking to?"

Back in the shop, Charlie took a deep breath.

"I know this is going to sound strange," he began.

But the cacophony of gunshots was building to a crescendo and pressing the receiver closer to her ear, Fiona frowned in annoyance before swapping it back to the other one.

"Sorry, missed all that. Tell me again, would you?"

Charlie took an even deeper breath and tried again.

"I repeat, I know this sounds strange but…"

It was still no good and, unable to hear a word, Fiona shouted to Fergus in frustration, "This is impossible."

Before she knew it, the footman had placed the salver over her hat encasing her entire head inside the dome. For his part, Charlie was struggling to remain calm too.

"Acknowledge situation impossible, but true."

"What situation?" persisted Fiona.

By this point the ghost was getting agitated also.

"Tell her you need to speak to her in person," he barked.

"Hello? Are you still there?" the Land Girl interjected in what she hoped was an appropriate pause as, yet again, she strained to hear the voice at the other end. She peeked under the rim of the dome at all the activity around her before lowering it again. She couldn't stand there all day, there were so many other things she had to do, but all the same she didn't want to ring off abruptly either, so acting on impulse as usual, she said the only thing she could think of on the spur of the moment. "Look, why not come to the party, everyone else is. We can talk then."

Charlie was deeply puzzled by the booming characteristic the woman's voice had assumed inside the metal dome and he frowned as he wrote the word that he thought he recognised as being *party* down in his book. Reading this, the ghost began to grin, which Charlie took to be an encouraging sign.

"Was that *party*?" he queried into the receiver.

"The last hurrah," Fiona replied, relieved to have finally conveyed some information successfully.

"What's the dress code for the last… for this party? Is it come as you are, or…?"

At that moment, a hearty guest with a particularly loud voice began bellowing to Angus, "I say, these coloured jobs are bloody marvellous, aren't they? Can actually see what I'm aiming at for a change."

No sooner had he belted up than the scruffy boys arrived and tapped respectfully on top of her dome. Lifting the lid, she was horrified to see them offering up a delicate vase as potential gun fodder.

"No, not that," she gasped, "it's seventeenth century!" She then pointed to a suitable alternative as Fergus shooed the boys back to the house.

"Seventeenth-century costume," Charlie spoke the words as he scrawled them. It was all so frustratingly cryptic but, as Caird was nodding enthusiastically, the repairman could only assume these fragments made more sense to the ghost than they did to him.

"What?" Fiona had just returned her attention back to the phone once more.

But then Fergus, who had been watching the skies with the polite pretence of not eavesdropping, suddenly began to yell the word "Cover!" Before she knew it, he had pulled the dome off her head, tossed the phone and salver aside and thrown them both under the table. A split second later a shower of porcelain rained down all about them.

1944

Charlie shuddered as the sound of each gunshot exploded in his earphones. It was all too much and he dropped the receiver and tore off his headset with trembling hands.

*

Back in the shop, Charlie looked up and, noticing the way the ghost's eyes were boring into him, reluctantly picked up the telephone receiver, which was lying on the floor.

"Hello? Are you there? Over. Hello?" But there was no reply, nothing. Just one of those huge empty silences that seems all the more huge and all the more empty for following a barrage of noise. "She's gone," he said in a faraway voice.

Further north, as the crow and the phone line flies, Fiona was also slightly stunned as she emerged from beneath the table and reached for the receiver lying on the grass nearby.

"Hello. Hello?" she called before turning to Fergus. "He's gone."

Charlie reached up to replace the receiver on its cradle before slumping back down to the floor again.

"I can't go to a party," he said drawing his knees up to his chest and hugging them.

"Balderdash!" replied the ghost.

Charlie looked up at his visitor searchingly. "You've seen how it is. I'll end up making a right spectacle of myself."

The ghost suddenly seemed in two minds as to what to do next. He certainly wasn't going to crouch down and beg, but he sensed that giving orders from on high wasn't going to help much either, so he resumed his pacing.

"Surely you go out sometimes?"

Instead of answering, Charlie reached to pick up his pencil and as he leant over, the screwdriver fell out of his lapel pocket.

"What about groceries?" the ghost persisted.

Charlie replaced the pencil in his pocket but kept the screwdriver in his hand, toying with it.

"Margie does all the housekeeping now."

"Margie?"

"My sister."

"Does she live here too?"

"No. She has her own family to look after."

Thoughts of family stirred some inner resolve, and slowly he began to raise himself to a standing position. "After I came home, well, my wife, she just…couldn't." Reaching his full height he found himself face to face and less than two feet away from the ghost.

"So, you rot here all by yourself?" It almost seemed like Caird was trying to goad him.

"No."

"Don't tell me, you have a bloody cat!" Caird *was* goading him. No doubt about it.

"I resemble, I mean I…" Charlie's anger emboldened him to give the ghost a hard stare. The ghost, for his part, stared straight back for a moment before glancing down at his uniform. Inevitably, Charlie's eyes were drawn to the same spot and to his horror he realised that he had been jabbing the ghost's chest with the end of the screwdriver. Worse still, the point had gone straight through him and made contact with a power socket on the wall behind.

Immediately, there was a crackling sound and they both pulled away in time to see sparks shooting out of the fixture. "… I resent that remark," finished Charlie, still angry.

A split second later there was a loud bang and as they both ducked, a singed cat fell past them, its fur all on end.

"Ah, some spark at last," quipped the ghost.

"Very funny," Charlie snapped back. Looking round he saw the cat cowering by the door and ran over to comfort it. Caird looked at his watch and frowned.

"It wasn't meant to be a joke."

"What then?" asked Charlie as he stroked the twitching animal.

It was the ghost who was starting to get angry now. Being a dog person, he had never been fond of cats at the best of times and the fact Charlie seemed more concerned about this wretched creature's plight than his own was winding him up badly.

"How on earth, and I do use the phrase advisedly," he began, building up a head of steam, "can I be expected to put on some kind, *any kind* of show for my nearest and dearest, if you persist in behaving like a damp squib? Damn it all, man, they're just as useless as dead ones when you're in a hurry."

Charlie raked a shaky hand through his hair before turning to give the ghost an even harder stare than before. Whilst he didn't need reminding of his fragile mental state, surely he wasn't as dead as Charles Caird? Or was he? Strewth! Now that was a shocking thought. He allowed his eyes to drift from the cat onto the pantomime poster which was stuck to the lower half of the door beside him. "Some kind of show for my nearest and dearest," he repeated to himself. Somewhere in the recess of his mind he had a vague memory of sitting in a theatre and listening to someone shouting from the stage.

"You don't think I'm useless do you, boys and girls?"

And beside him his nephew and his nieces had all shouted back, "No!"

"I can't hear you," the voice from the stage had cried again.

And that time the whole auditorium, himself included, had answered with a resounding "*No!*"

"Really shout it this time," exhorted the character on the stage, and, at a deafening pitch, the answer came back emphatically for a third time, "*Noooooo!*"

Very carefully he peeled the poster off the door, walked back to the counter and placed it face side up. "Theatre will have some costumes, I reckon," he said quietly.

"Now you're talking," said Caird, greatly encouraged and not a little surprised by the change of attitude.

"Normally they just offer us complimentary tickets in return for the use of our window, but perhaps they'd stretch to something bigger this time."

"Then let's get them stretching," replied the ghost before realising the radio repairman was already on his way back to the kitchen.

"Like Widow Twankey's knicker elastic, there's an awful lot hanging on it," he quipped whilst hurrying to catch up.

Chapter Five

Ivan and Lady Caird were returning to the fringes of the shooting party when a piece of china landed at the man's feet.

"What the hell is that?" he barked in surprise.

"Spode," said his aunt as she bent down to examine it more carefully.

"China!" expostulated Ivan.

"Yes, one of the saucers Aunt Muriel gave us. They were part of a wedding present," she replied, before a mischievous look crept into her eye. "I never did like them much. At least Fiona was clever enough to find another use for them at last, and so much cheaper than those expensive clays, don't you think?"

"Clever? It's wanton destruction!"

"Oh, do stop being so melodramatic," said Lady Caird, hoping she didn't sound quite as weary as she felt.

"Why does everyone around here get so defensive when I ask them a simple question?" Ivan continued, just as cross as ever.

Lady Caird, as has already been noted, was a tolerant

woman, but she well knew that some people could be like dogs when they got hold of a bone, or bone china as the case may be. The fact that Ivan was the son of her husband's poorer brother only served to make things more difficult, but who else was in a position to scold him?

"Perhaps, dear nephew, it's because they've just spent six very long years, all mucking in together, trying to keep this little community in trust for when the war was over. And, now that it is, losing a stake in its future must seem a like a very bitter betrayal indeed."

Chapter Six

CHARLIE WAS HURRYING ACROSS THE YARD carrying a picnic basket when the ghost called after him from the house.

"There's a note on this door saying it shouldn't be left open. Looks like a woman's writing."

"That'll be Margie, she's always leaving notes, so I don't forget things," Charlie shouted back as he reached a pair of sliding doors that fronted an outbuilding.

"She must get writer's cramp," muttered the ghost as he tried to pull the kitchen door closed behind him. However, he found he could no more hold a door handle than a telephone.

Charlie meanwhile had opened the doors to reveal a dusty van with an enormous speaker on its roof.

"She's a good old girl really and you're another, aren't you my beauty?" He stroked the bonnet before walking round to the driver's door and climbing inside. The smell of leather was balm for his soul and he inhaled deeply whilst pulling out the choke and turning the ignition. It took a couple of goes, but the engine soon fired up without too much bother. Evidently someone had been keeping the battery charged. Charlie patted the dashboard in gratitude and steered the vehicle out into the yard where the ghost was waiting for him.

"What the hell is that?" he asked as Charlie jumped down from the cab, "Some kind of tank?"

"Our dauntless, dependable delivery vehicle," the repairman replied, knowing full well that a bit of alliteration, like a bit of rhyme, doesn't come amiss in stories such as this.

Caird, who had no time for either, merely jabbed his finger in the direction of the back door to the house. Surprisingly, it was enough for Charlie to recall the duty he must perform there and he returned to make the building secure. The ghost watched and wondered. There were moments when this man could be perfectly quick on the uptake and yet so damnably slow at others. Somehow the contrast helped him begin to grasp the enormity of the damage done. In the First World War, they would have called Charlie's condition battle fatigue. In fact, he had used the term himself, but now it seemed completely inadequate, insulting even. As if a week by the sea would sort it out. Even if some chap, unfortunate enough to be so labelled, could afford a holiday, the condition was obviously too complicated to be treated so simply. Better than nothing, perhaps, but scarcely long enough to unravel a tangled mind. That would take a whole lot more. More than damned screwdrivers and soldering irons. He smiled at the ridiculousness of the image whilst glimpsing the relationship between useful activity and recovery. The repairman was back beside him now, running a hand along the side of this monstrous vehicle and revealing the painted lettering beneath the dust. And how much happier he seemed while he was about it.

"At least someone had the gumption to check the battery and keep an eye on the engine," Caird said out loud, and he could've sworn the repairman stood a little taller when he heard it.

"Taking it out on the road might be good for business. Margie would like that," Charlie said quietly.

"She believes in keeping up appearances then?"

"Aye, she's a bit like you in that respect."

"Was that a joke? Asked the ghost in surprise.

Charlie smiled for the first time before opening the passenger door for Caird and shutting it for him afterwards. Once he was in his own seat, he raised the revs to a robust throaty rumble, put the gear in first and pulled away.

"We could play *I Spy*," said Caird, relieved to be moving at last. But no sooner had the words left his lips than Charlie braked suddenly.

"I've forgotten something, haven't I?" he groaned. "Something really important." His brow furrowed as he tried to remember. "Something beginning with *w*."

"If you say *windscreen*, I'll brain you," said the ghost, fuming again.

"No, that's not it," interrupted Charlie as he peered past his passenger and up at the house. "And I shut all the windows," he muttered going through a visual security check at the same time. "W, w, w—"

It was now the ghost's turn to interrupt, "Are they an honest lot around here?"

"As the day is long," replied Charlie, aghast anyone should ask such a question about his home county.

For his own part, any satisfaction the ghost might have taken from provoking regional pride to further his own ends was offset by the pressing need for progress. "Then let's get this bloody show on the road!"

Chapter Seven

IT WAS PERHAPS HALF AN HOUR LATER WHEN Marge entered the kitchen. Well, at least her brother hadn't left the back door open, she thought, as she ushered in her brood. Because it was the school holidays, she had the full contingent that morning, not just Albert and the little 'un, but the two older girls too. She put her basket down on the table and noticed the unused place setting from the night before.

"Why I bother leaving him notes, I just don't know."

Smelling the air inevitably led to the discovery of the burnt saucepan in the sink.

"Jean, find the soda crystals and put them in this saucepan to soak, and Janet, you keep an eye on your brothers for me while I go and find Uncle Charlie." The two girls did as they were told while their mother journeyed into the interior.

As she peered into the workshop, her eyes fell first on the empty stool and then the army radio set beside it, strangely alive now with all its dials glowing. The cat stirred lazily from its perch on top and watched as the woman exited again.

After a quick glance into the shop, she hurried to the foot of the staircase and called up. "Charlie love, you're not ill are yer?"

Getting no response, she began to climb the narrow staircase and knocked on a door at the top.

"I didn't mean for that business yesterday to bring on your old trouble. Honestly I didn't."

She pressed her ear against the woodwork but still there was no answer, not even the sound of breathing. "Charlie?"

Bustling into the room, she found the curtains wide open and cold morning light slanting in. Those December rays, weak though they were, were enough to reveal a bed that had not been slept in and the spines of numerous books on the nightstand. Distractedly, she picked one up as if it might contain a clue as to her brother's whereabouts, but it was only a rhyming dictionary. She almost smiled at the sight. Who else but Charlie would bother reading one of those? A Charlie she now couldn't find. Slapping the book down again she hurried over to the window, which afforded a view of the yard below. From her vantage point she could see that the doors to one of the outbuildings were open. The fact that they were sliding doors and didn't open outwards meant that one could easily enter the yard without noticing them, just as she had done when she'd arrived. Not only were they open but the van from inside had gone too.

Reaching the foot of the stairs, Marge checked the row of coat pegs. Just as she expected, a man's coat and scarf still hung in its usual place. From there it was just a couple of paces back through the strip curtain and into the retail space. She glanced at the clock on the wall. It was 9 am and whether her brother was missing or not, that meant *opening up time.*

Undoing the bolts on the front door she noticed an empty space where the pantomime poster had been. Walking back to the counter she pondered on what it all meant. Then, almost mechanically, she opened the order book, reached for the phone and began to dial.

Saunders was sitting with the phone against his ear and a box of personal effects on the desk before him. Apart from the chair and the desk there was one green metal filing cabinet and four blank white walls. It suited him just fine. A new office and a new start, even if it was the same old job. He had only got his demob a month earlier but had been restless to rejoin the force, and the force, for its part, had been anxious to have him back. He didn't know what he would've done if they hadn't. Policing was all he'd known since he was eighteen and had worked his way up to Detective Inspector. He was one of the lucky ones, as he knew, with an understanding wife and two healthy, happy kids. But though he seemed to have been able to pick up the pieces of civilian life pretty easily, he appreciated others had not and that was likely to cause complications later on. The kind of complications that started when fundamentally decent men were drawn into petty crime in order to make ends meet. He pulled out a framed photo as he listened to the voice on the other end of the receiver.

"Put her on," he said at last and blew the dust off the picture. "How are things?"

Marge glanced at the army radio telephone which she could just make out behind the strip curtain.

"The lights are on, but no one's home," she said.

"How's that?" Saunders asked, putting the family portrait down.

"The set! Your set, it looks like it's mended now, but Charlie…"

He could sense her trying to fight back her emotions.

"I think I need to report a missing person."

Chapter Eight

ALL JOURNEYS OF DISCOVERY REQUIRE A journey, and if they involve physical effort as well, so much the better. Distance matters. How can you come a long way, if you haven't come a long way?

It was perhaps fortunate then that Caird's family home was up in Scotland. Starting from northern England meant that heading east or west wouldn't have really amounted to much, the country being just too narrow at that point. That only left north or south. South just meant more of England so, in order for Charles and Charlie to have the truly transformative experience fantastic stories require, they really only had the one option, to head north.

As they had been travelling for quite a while, Charlie pulled to a halt on a high moorland plateau. It was an exposed spot but atmospheric and both travellers got out to stretch their legs. Whilst Caird was content to drink in the scenery, Charlie ambled over with the picnic basket. Sitting down on a slab of rock he removed a flask and a couple of parcels wrapped in greaseproof paper. He was just about to offer one to the ghost when a thought crossed his mind. The only knowledge he had of ghosts had come from folk legends and popular culture, but it struck him then that, in each case, the unfortunate spirit was given a unique characteristic. Hadn't Stanley Holloway recounted Ann Boleyn's particular ability in the monologue 'With Her Head Tucked Underneath Her Arm'?[6] In that respect, he concluded, ghosts should be treated as individuals rather than lumped together in one spectral mass. And, whilst it was in his nature to share, he had no wish to witness his companion spurting like a sieve.

"Can you eat and drink in your condition?" he asked carefully.

"I bloody hope so," answered the ghost just as doubt began to enter his own mind. He looked around, almost as if seeking permission from somewhere or something. "After all," he continued in a quieter tone, "even condemned men are allowed a hearty breakfast, aren't they?"

If the ghost's special pleading prompted an answer, Charlie couldn't tell, but when Caird spoke again he was back to his hearty self. "What's on offer?"

"Tart."

"Are you advertising?"

"Only the Bakewell," said Charlie, ignoring the double entendre. "It was meant for last night's supper but in all the… er… confusion, it was forgotten."

The ghost chuckled before reaching out for a slice and to his great relief found he could hold it.

"Seems like you've been granted some special powers after all," observed Charlie.

---

6   Lyrics by R.P. Weston and Bert Lee, music by Harris Weston, first published in 1934, © Sony/ATV Music Publishing LLC.

"Just the one I think," said Caird as he tore off the paper and took a bite.

Charlie watched thoughtfully. "Your ability to transmogrify food takes consumption onto quite another plane."

"And what plane would that be?" asked the ghost with his mouth full.

"The plain pastry!" replied Charlie with a note of triumph.

"Hah, and it sounds like you've just swallowed the dictionary."

"But that's the right word, isn't it?" stammered Charlie, suddenly crushed along with his bon mot.

"I mean you have to be precise with language otherwise mistakes hap…" His voice trailed away and he shivered involuntarily, something that the ghost, even in the midst of his feeding frenzy, was sensitive enough to notice. His bluster, like all behaviours, had been learnt, in his case probably in the nursery, and whilst it had tended to be the default position throughout his life, he'd come to realise it was going to be of limited use from here on in, or in the hereafter, or wherever it was.

"Of course you have, old chap," he resumed adopting a more mollifying tone. "Didn't mean to criticise, just my clumsy way of alluding to your impressive vocabulary, that's all. No doubt the fruits of much admirable reading and study." He paused a moment before continuing. "I only wish I'd read more. I wish I'd done a lot of things, but it's too late now."

Much to the ghost's surprise, the radio repairman did not seem at all placated by the new approach for, when he spoke, his voice was bitter with self-recrimination and he was trembling too.

"And don't you see that by saying that you're only making matters worse?"

The ghost didn't see; all he knew he was that he was going to have to try harder.

Chapter Nine

FIONA SAT AT ONE END OF THE TABLE QUARTERING apples with Martha, whilst Angus stood at the other end trying to referee between Cameron and the scruffy boys as to whose turn it was to stir the punch bowl. Although Cameron was at a distinct disadvantage being both younger and smaller than the other two, his father did his best to maintain fair play. Fortunately, at that moment, distraction appeared in the form of their Uncle Fergus who entered carrying a wooden crate. It was enough for all the youngsters to instantly run to his side. Even the adults stopped what they were doing, including Lady Caird and Amy who had been preparing haggis over by the sideboard. Satisfied he had their full attention, Fergus pulled a layer of blue tissue paper from the top of the crate with all the panache of a magician.

"Ta-dah!" he trumpeted as an abundance of bright-orange oranges was revealed underneath. "I've been keeping these hidden under my bed."

"Good gracious, Fergus, are they real?" gasped Lady Caird once the initial shock had passed.

"A cousin of ours works at the docks in Glasgow and these kind of fell off the back of a freighter," he beamed.

"The cousin is the black sheep of the family," Amy added quickly, sensing her Ladyship may not have subscribed to the *finders-keepers* philosophy.

"There's one in every family," her Ladyship noted ruefully.

"And they're not the only ones to grow woolly coats, Ma'am. I bet that little lot are covered in them," interjected Angus.

"They're not mouldy," retorted Fergus. "I've eaten one already and no side effects at all."

Angus winked at Fiona, "Well there must be something wrong with them or you wouldnae be sharing them with us now, would you?"

"And aren't you my family too?" the footman replied with feeling. "Besides I thought they'd come in handy for the punch."

"Making marmalade used to be quite a forte of mine," mused Lady Caird with a misty look in her eye.

"Even if we could get the sugar, I doubt we'd be here long enough to enjoy it," Fiona replied gently.

"No, I suppose not," sighed the old lady as she was brought back to the present with a jolt.

"We could try making squash," piped Amy.

Lady Caird smiled indulgently but Fergus groaned.

"It's not a Sunday School outing, woman," snapped Angus, for once siding with his brother.

Amy, though small and seemingly timid, was capable of assuming quite indomitable moral superiority on occasion, particularly where her children were concerned

52

and, as she felt this was one of those occasions, she straightened every inch of her five-foot frame before answering him. "I'm well aware of that, Angus McPherson, but I'll not have our children consuming strong liquor."

Angus knew better than to argue with his wife at such times, in fact, deep down, he recognised the dangerous cycle of sons repeating the behaviour of their fathers. That he had been able to escape it himself was partly due to her steely influence. The fact that she had been willing to up sticks and join him at the castle, bringing the children with her, was still further evidence of her strength of character and the reason they could now live together as a family in such spacious surroundings. That said, someone still had to make a decision about the oranges and, as was so often the case, it fell to Fiona to be that person.

"Why don't we just make both?" she asked lightly. "There's enough there. All those in favour say aye."

The "ayes" carried it.

Fergus put the crate on the table and Fiona ceremonially handed him her knife. "Start slicing a few but don't do them all," she instructed before bowling several oranges to Amy who, laughing, caught them in her apron. "You know, this has just given me an idea for fancy dress," she added before darting out of the room.

Chapter Ten

MARGE WAS STANDING BY THE COAT HOOKS at the foot of the stairs.

"See, he didn't even take his winter coat with him."

Saunders could see all right, but he let her continue.

"There's only an old mackintosh in the van and that's not a bit of use against the cold, particularly if he's stuck out on the moors somewhere. And the way he is now he wouldn't even think to put it on anyway."

She caught herself, folded the coat carefully over her arm and led the policeman into the kitchen. Once there she indicated Saunders should take a seat whilst she transferred the coat on to the back of a spare chair, treating it just like a personage in itself. Setting herself down she picked up the toddler, Henry, and dangled him on her knee. Meanwhile, Jean handed the policeman a cup, which Janet filled from a brown teapot.

"I've alerted the force to keep an eye out," Saunders said once the girls had moved away.

"But don't *you* have an idea where he might have gone?" the woman asked in surprise.

The policeman examined the oil cloth table covering for a moment before answering. "You knew the plan: try and jog Charlie into remembering the family name so we could trace an address and travel there together."

"Seems like he may have gone and done it all by himself."

"He can't." The policeman's tone was much more matter-of-fact now. "A verbal will requires two witnesses for it to be valid. I checked on the legality of it all as soon as I got the chance. We were both there when it was made, we both have to be there when it's delivered."

"So now we're a brother *and* a witness short," said Marge shifting Henry onto her other knee.

"From where I was standing, I'm sure I picked up the trace of a Scottish accent, so Charlie, being that much closer to the fallen man, would definitely have been able to do the same. Of course, that doesn't mean our mystery soldier lived north of the border, but without contacting every Highland regiment, even assuming their records were up to date…"

"But if you and Charlie were both in the Yorkshires, what were you doing with Highland troops anyway?"

Saunders shifted slightly in his seat. Whilst talking about his wartime experience was not traumatic for him, he still found it difficult to explain things to people who had not seen active service. Delivering the facts unemotionally and without wasted description suited both his personality and the circumstances.

"In the chaos after the landings we'd got separated from our own unit, so we were mighty glad to tag along with anyone, and to hell with all the social introductions."

At that moment the shop bell rang and Albert, tasked with keeping watch, ran into the kitchen. "Customer," he shouted excitedly.

"You make an excellent lookout," Saunders told the boy as his mother rose to leave.

"Are we going to form a posse to find Uncle Charlie?" asked Albert, already eager for larger responsibilities.

Chapter Eleven

AIRD TACTFULLY LOOKED AWAY WHILE Charlie reached for the flask and shakily poured out two teas. He then took the cup the radio repairman offered him and pretended not to notice as Charlie spilt half the contents of his own cup into his lap.

"Told you I wasn't fit to go out, didn't I?" he groaned as he stood up to assess the damage.

Still feigning not to watch Charlie's embarrassed efforts to wipe away the stain, the ghost turned his attention towards the van instead. "You were steady enough behind the wheel though," he countered. "How about telling me about the origin of the species and pass the sugar while you're about it."

Charlie passed a twist of paper containing the sugar before following the direction of the ghost's gaze. "My father customised it himself."

"He must have been a clever man," the ghost continued, genuinely impressed. "That speaker alone must have taken some fitting."

"Aye, he was all of that," replied Charlie, beginning to forget his distress.

"What was it used for?"

"Elections mostly. Other times the old man would drive round playing the radio through it to try and coax people into the shop. Folks used to claim they could hear it in Barnsley."

Having finished his tea, the ghost wandered over to take a closer look at the equipment.

"Does it still work?"

"Course it does," Charlie replied indignantly.

Once they were both inside the cab and the engine was running, Charlie wiped the dust off the microphone and turned on the Tannoy.[7] Then he hesitated.

"Go on then, say something," urged the ghost.

"My mind's gone blank," said Charlie, his face matching his mental state.

There was a moment's delay and then his words bounced back off the hillside, "... blank, blank, blank."

"Bloody hell! It really does carry doesn't it? Try something else?"

"No, I feel daft."

Another moment's delay and his words echoed back a second time "... daft, daft, daft."

"Well, you get the idea anyway," Charlie said, switching the speaker off again.

"From now on I'm calling you Charlie Echo," announced his delighted passenger.

"Ho, ho, ho," retorted the repairman, unamused.

"See, you can't help yourself," persisted the ghost.

"Charlie Echo," muttered Charlie dismissively as he eased off the hand brake and started to pull away. "Sure you don't mean second fiddle?"

---

7   The trademark for an electrical public address system.

58

"Very droll," replied Caird, who was not to be cast down so easily. "Though some music would be nice. It would make the miles go faster, too, don't you think?"

Charlie twiddled the tuning knob until he hit upon a song. 'I'm An Old Cowhand (From The Rio Grande)' Crosby crooned into the cab.[8]

"Will that do you?"

"And through the speaker?"

Shaking his head, Charlie flicked the switch and his passenger began to sing along with the tune whilst listening for the echo through the open window. "... *I'm a riding fool who is up to date, I know every trail in the Lone Star State, 'cause I ride the range in a Ford V8...*" When it got to the chorus the ghost looked at Charlie willing him to join in which, reluctantly, he did.

"... *yippie yi yo kayah,*" they sang together in variable harmony.

As the van followed the contours of the road, higher up still, a policeman was leaning on his bicycle having a crafty gasper.[9] He often used this mode of transport when visiting remote farms in the area, though any health benefits from energetic pedalling were probably cancelled out by his smoking habit. Still, it was a grand feeling to have the moors to oneself on such a clear morning, a spot where there was nothing to disturb him... except the sound of a radio! Scanning the horizon he could see no

---

8   'I'm An Old Cowhand (From The Rio Grande)' Words and Music by Jonny Mercer (c) 1936, The Johnny Mercer Foundation (ASCAP). All rights administered by WC Music Corp. Originally recorded and popularised by Bing Crosby. Many years later Harry Connick Jr performed a notable cover version.

9   "Gasper", British Army slang for a high-tar cigarette without any kind of filter, such as a Woodbine or Capstone.

one approaching, from any direction. The only moving thing within a mile's radius was a delivery vehicle way down below, but surely there was no way a thing so far away could produce a sound so close. But, as the vehicle drew nearer, he began to make out an enormous conical horned speaker attached to the roof and inside one man mouthing the words to the song he could hear so clearly.

"*We're old cow hands from the Rio Grande,*
and we've come to town just to hear the band.
We know every song that the cowboys know…"

Stubbing out his cigarette, the policeman grabbed his bike and began pedalling downhill in hot pursuit.

Back inside the cab the ghost looked at Charlie again, defying him not to recognise the significance of the next line, "*… 'bout the big corral where the doggies go, we learned them all off the radio…*"

Charlie got the joke all right and by the time the next chorus came around both men were singing with gusto.

Unlike the policeman, we of course, have the added advantage of being able to skip between two places in less time than it takes to sing *Yippe yi yo kayah*, and so can recognise the difference between two men singing together inside a cab and one man singing solo, which was all that the copper could discern from outside of it. Either way, he was sure that the racket breached some by law or other, and as he was just close enough to make out the name on the van's side and its number plate, he stopped and noted them down.

Chapter Twelve

FINLAY WAS HELPING LADY CAIRD LOAD BOOKS into a tea chest. The fact that there were far more books on the shelves than in the chest indicated two things: firstly that they were in the library, and secondly that they had barely begun packing. Meanwhile, Fiona was sitting near the window mending an old dress. Judging by the pale light outside it was already mid-afternoon and, although a modest fire was burning in the hearth, the pervading atmosphere was one of gloom, as it often is on the last day of the year. Getting to the end of a line of stitching, the Land Girl snapped the thread between her teeth, causing Lady Caird to glance over.

"And where on earth did you dig that old thing out from?" she asked.

"The dressing-up trunk in the attic; you don't mind?"

"Why should I? I can't even begin to face the thought of trying to clear up there as well," the old lady said as she slumped onto the sofa. "I'm getting old, Finlay, that's what it is."

Following her lead, Finlay went and sat down beside her.

"Age has nothing to do with it," he said diplomatically. "Just a normal impulse to push unpleasant tasks to the back of one's mind in the hope that they'll go away."

"But they never do, do they?" reflected Lady Caird sadly.

Fiona put down her sewing, "Do you think that's the reason Charles didn't leave a will?"

Caught in the cross-beam, Finlay took his time to answer. As the family solicitor for more years than he could remember, he desperately wanted to help these two women but, as he was also scrupulously honest, he couldn't profess to understanding something that he did not.

"Whenever I raised the subject with your fiancé, he'd just smile and reel off a list of all the Cairds who'd returned unscathed after various battles throughout history."

"Statistics as an illusion of mastery," sighed Lady Caird.

Fiona gave a quizzical sideways glance at Charles's portrait.

"Or just plain tardiness," she observed. "There's a whole lot more mastery in writing things down, and I'd damn well tell him to do so. If I had the chance, that is."

"Certainly," Finlay continued, as his mind searched for some explanation, "but for some, I can only speculate as to whether Charles was among their number, it may only be in the midst of battle that they finally start to understand what they value in life and most want to perpetuate at home."

"Too late, too late," Lady Caird sighed again.

Chapter Thirteen

MARGE WAS BEHIND THE SHOP COUNTER surrounded by her four children, whilst Saunders was on the phone. The repaired W.S. 18 loomed large between them.

"Ah, excellent," she could hear the policeman saying. "And was he detained?"

She shot a glance at the man, hardly daring to hope, but she should've known things were not going to work out quite that easily. As should we.

"No, I see. Well, that would be too much to hope for I suppose." He turned around and caught her quizzical expression. "Yes, Sergeant, and you. Thanks for keeping me informed."

How strange they took the trouble to exchange New Year greetings at a time like this, she thought, as her mind filled in the pauses.

Saunders put the phone down carefully, buying himself extra thinking time.

"The van's been sighted heading north," he said at last.

"Scotland?"

"Early indications suggest so."

"When a Yorkshireman's sure of a thing, he stays sure."

"If we wait a while longer, I'll expect we'll get confirmation he's crossed the border."

"And if we left now, we might still catch him and avert another tragedy," she replied firmly.

"If *we* left?"

"That's right. Family is family and this is a family business." She glanced at the young heads bobbing around her. "Besides, there's no time to find minders for this little lot and their father'll be wanting his beer just the same. Get your coats on, children, we're going on an outing."

She then strode over to the front door and bolted it with a finality that settled the matter.

Chapter Fourteen

THE VAN CREPT DOWN THE GRAVEL DRIVE THAT led to Caird Castle, whilst up ahead several cars were disgorging guests. That Charlie could discern as much was due to a brightly illuminated porch-cum-portico, directly ahead.

"You needn't drive all the way up to the house," the ghost said helpfully.

"*House*, he says!" came the exclamation from the driver's seat. "Talk about misleading information."

"If we bear to the right, we can leave the van in the old coach house. It'll be less conspicuous there and you can change in one of the stalls."

"Roger that," answered Charlie, only too happy to steer away from the hubbub and make for the obscurity beyond. But all too soon he found himself walking back the way he had come. As his eyes adjusted from the outer darkness to the brightness within, he could make out a red carpet leading up from the portico into the heart of the building. *Like the lolling tongue of a sleeping beast*, he thought. Talk about putting your head inside a lion's mouth. There was a monologue about that too, and in 'The Lion and Albert', it hadn't ended well for Albert either.[10]

The grim stoicism of the tale had always amused him. So much so that he had suggested Margie name her oldest boy after it. In an alternative comedy universe, he could just imagine her speculating about how much she could get for the poor lad's clothes. Clothes! His mind seemed to pop at the notion for, at the self-same moment that his subconscious was recalling this bit of comedy trivia, his conscious mind was presenting him with something altogether more startling: the guests were in ordinary evening dress! Not just one, but all of them! Horrified at the sartorial embarrassment that was about to confront him, Charlie spun on his heel only to bump into Fergus instead.

"Your mackintosh, sir?" asked the footman, holding out a gloved hand.

"Er no, I think I'll keep it on, thanks," Charlie mumbled before ducking out of reach and retreating back into the shadows again. Then he pulled the collar of the mac up over his mouth so passers-by wouldn't see his lips move.

"I can't go in there," he said turning to the ghost.

"Why the hell not?"

"All the men are in bloody black tie!"

The ghost looked up and chuckled. "So they bloody are," he agreed.

"Oh aye, you can laugh all right, but it's Muggins here who has to play the court jester."

"It's a party, the joke's on them for being so straight-laced."

10   'The Lion and Albert', Marriot Edgar, published by F. Day and Hunter, 1931.

But Charlie was not to be buttered up so easily.

"I could've sworn she said 'seventeenth century'. I wrote it down. You saw me do it."

Caird tried to place a restraining hand on Charlie's shoulder, then remembered he couldn't.

Even so, the radio repairman twisted away violently. "Leave me alone," he shouted, causing two approaching guests to stare in surprise. But Charlie was now in such a funk that he didn't even notice.

Lost in his inner turmoil, he strode back towards the coach house and the ghost had to run to catch up. Even from several paces behind, Caird could not only see Charlie gesticulating to himself but hear his muttering too.

"How can I deliver a will correctly if I can't even get a party invitation right? The whole idea's bonkers."

On reaching the coach house, Charlie yanked one of the doors open and stormed inside before turning to face his pursuer. "You don't need me for this," he steamed.

"I don't?" asked the ghost feigning surprise.

"You need someone who can hold a thought in their head for longer than two seconds and who has the confidence to express themselves in a clear and forthright manner."

"I see," replied the ghost evenly as he watched Charlie climb into the van and turn on the ignition. The engine caught first time and a split second later, the headlights were on too. The situation was changing rapidly, much too rapidly for his liking. If he didn't do something very soon, all would be lost. But the lights might just help. Taking advantage of the extra illumination, the ghost scanned the interior, his eyes running along the shelves and bits of old riding tack until they settled on a petrol can. He had no idea if it was full or empty, but desperate times required desperate measures, so he hurried round to the front of the van and shouted above the engine noise.

"Might be an idea to top her up before you go, don't you think?" Charlie eyed him suspiciously, before getting out of the cab again. Further hard stares were interspersed between Charlie unscrewing the cap to the fuel tank and the retrieval of the petrol can. As soon as Charlie had his back turned, Caird unwrapped a twist of paper from his pocket and ran towards the rear of the vehicle.

"What are you doing?"

"Just putting some sugar in your petrol tank."

"Say that again?" the repairman asked incredulously.

"There's nothing wrong with your hearing, Charlie Echo."

Charlie ran over and dropped the can at his feet. He wanted to hit the ghost but knowing he couldn't, he kicked the can instead.

"You miserable bit of mouldering miasma," he spluttered.

"Very forthrightly put," replied the ghost approvingly.

"That's sabotage!"

"Isn't that what you've been doing to yourself for the last five minutes?" asked the ghost gently.

They stared each other down for several seconds before Charlie stomped to the back of the van and opened the rear doors.

"You'll not stop me from changing out of these ridiculous clothes at any rate," he shouted as he reached inside for a paper bag. But no sooner had he peered inside than he began to groan again.

"What's the matter now?" asked the ghost who was wisely keeping his distance.

"My trousers, they're all stained from that hot tea I spilt."

"Ah, stewed plums, eh? Very nasty," came a knowing voice from the front of the vehicle.

"It's in the worst spot, right enough."

"Between a rock and a hard place, you might say."

"I wouldn't, but Max Miller might,"[11] Charlie called back as he hurled the paper bag inside the van again.

"What *is* the difference between a ghost and a comedian, I wonder?"

"I don't know, and I don't care" said Charlie slamming the door, which refused to close.

"A ghost can't die on stage," answered the ghost, tickled by his own wit.

Charlie slammed the door again; same thing. Finally, he hurled himself at the obstinate object in a frenzy of frustration and this time it worked, but the effort had left him so close to tears that he scrunched his eyes shut.

---

11   Max Miller, 1894–1963, otherwise known as 'The Cheeky Chappie', was widely regarded as the greatest British stand-up comedian of his generation.

Chapter Fifteen

SAUNDERS' LITTLE AUSTIN 7 BEETLED ALONG THE moorland road. In the gathering gloom, the scene looked far less appealing than it had earlier in the day and, despite the cramped interior, none of the passengers would have thought of stopping there. Saunders was at the wheel, Marge, in the passenger seat, and Albert, although nominally seated in the back, was leaning so far forward that his head was tucked between the adults. Jean and Janet, meanwhile, were on the back seat on either side of Albert. Janet was holding Henry and Jean was trying to pass a cup of tea over to her mother, who was staring straight ahead.

"Yee-ha, yee-ha!" yelled Albert repeatedly, convinced he was driving a team of six horses across the plains.

"If you say that one more time, I'm going to pour this all over your head," snapped Jean, "and then it'll be 'tea-hee, tea-hee."

Albert was unperturbed. "If we don't find Uncle Charlie soon, the trail will go cold. Isn't that right?" he said turning to Saunders.

"Then let's just hope some friendly settlers offer him shelter for the night," the policeman replied, exchanging a worried glance with Marge.

Chapter Sixteen

CHARLIE HAD HIS EYES FIRMLY CLOSED AGAIN as two hands reached out to take his coat. There was nothing for it now but to turn sideways and allow the hands, which belonged to Fergus, to take hold of the mackintosh. The hands were all too efficient and, with scarcely a moment's delay, Charlie's outer garment was removed, revealing the pantomime costume underneath.

"Welcome to Castle Caird, sir," said Fergus without mockery and, as Charlie blinked and examined the footman more closely, it occurred to him that perhaps he wasn't the only one in costume after all. Here, at least, was a comrade at arms. Then he became conscious of all the other staring faces and felt outnumbered again.

He turned to the ghost who was standing to his left.

"Eyes front," Caird ordered and an old reflex made Charlie obey, despite himself. When the instruction to "Move forward" came, he did that too.

In pure pantomime terms this would have been called the *transformation scene*, the scene where both audience and characters are presented with another world. In fact, there was a time when not just the scenery but the characters themselves transformed and would have been played by other performers, the whole process becoming a Harlequinade.[12] But that did not happen here. Charlie was still recognisably Charlie, and although he felt sickeningly self-conscious on the inside, walking purposefully made him appear purposeful and any impulse to snigger people may have had was stifled. It is also important to remember that seventeenth-century costume included clothes worn by both Roundheads and Cavaliers, honest yeoman and reckless buccaneers, and something of both these extremes attached themselves to the radio repairman as he advanced up the stairway.

The ghost, meanwhile, ambled up easily along behind, easily that is until he saw the three people in the receiving line. Ivan was the first, Lady Caird next and then Fiona, who was dressed as Nell Gwyn.[13]

"A friend of Fiona's, I assume," scowled Ivan, taking in the costume as Charlie drew level with him.

"Well, we've never actually met, but…"

"Yet another freeloader," the little man retorted.

"Ivan!" Lady Caird rebuked her nephew.

Ivan ignored her and turned his disapproving gaze onto the next arrival.

Well, that went well, thought Charlie as he took another

---

12   Alexander Sullivan, Jill, *The Politics Of Pantomime, Regional Identity In The Theatre*, University of Hertfordshire, 2011, p33

13   Eleanor Gwyn, more commonly known as Nell Gwyn, was a notable figure in Restoration England, famous for being a seller of oranges, an accomplished comedy actress and last, but by no means least, for being the mistress of King Charles II of England, Scotland and Wales.

pace forward and this time he was greeted by Lady Caird's smile.

"So pleased you could come, Mr… ?"

"Goodman," said Charlie taking her hand.

"Mr Goodman," she repeated warmly before continuing. "And it's so nice to see you've dressed up as well. We always used to have fancy dress parties in the old days. We had a lot more staff then too of course, but the older ones got older and retired and the younger ones volunteered or got called up. Some come back, but others…" Her gaze drifted away to a place just beyond Charlie's left shoulder. Turning to locate her point of interest, Charlie realised she was now looking directly at Caird, and the ghost, for his part, was looking right back at his mother. He lifted his arms to embrace her then, remembering his moribund state, let them flop down again. Charlie couldn't help but notice that the old lady's face was now wearing a very troubled expression and he wasn't the only one to register the change.

"What's the matter?" Fiona whispered.

"I just had the strangest feeling…" replied Lady Caird after a pause during which the ghost moved around to Charlie's other side, "but it's passed now."

"You've been standing too long."

Lady Caird merely waved away her concern and, knowing how much the old lady hated fuss, Fiona decided not to press the issue. Instead, she turned her attention to the man in the fancy-dress costume who was now standing before her.

"Fiona Maclean, of no fixed status," she said executing a little curtsey and stealing a sideway glance at Ivan at the same time. With her eyes momentarily averted, Charlie studied both the girl and her costume with interest.

"Were you the person I phoned this morning?" he stammered. "You sounded so different on the blower."

It was now the girl's turn to give him the once-over. "It would appear so, wouldn't it?"

"I've got my wires horribly crossed," he murmured apologetically.

"No, no. My fault entirely. Trying to do too many things at once as usual. It's fatal isn't it?"

The lightness of her tone wrong-footed him.

"Confusion reigns," he conceded.

Yet still she seemed to want to hold him in conversation. Was it just to compensate for the mix-up that morning, he wondered?

"It's like that message that starts out as *send reinforcements we're going to advance* and ends up as *send four and sixpence we're going to a dance*," she giggled.

"Don't joke about it, *please!*"

She registered the almost physical pain behind the words and the change in her tone was as sudden as it was altered.

"Come on, we'll go into the kitchen and get some Dutch courage. I know I could do with some."

"That's my girl," said the ghost as the two men followed her through an archway and down into the bowels of the castle.

As unobtrusively as he could, Charlie held the swing door open, allowing the ghost to pass through before following him down the stone steps to the kitchen.

"We've got a bowl of punch in the hall, but you look

like you could do with something stronger, am I right?" asked the girl as she went over to the table.

The radio repairman nodded and watched her sort through the bottles.

"I'm glad you came, Mr Goodman. I'd have ended up looking like a proper lemon if you hadn't, wouldn't I?" She glanced at the oranges in the basket slung over her arm, "Sorry, wrong fruit, but you know what I mean."

"You could never be mistaken for a lemon."

"Why, thank you."

She was just moving over to the sideboard when she passed the apparently empty space where the ghost was standing. Caird made no attempt at hugs this time, just settling for a snatched air kiss instead.

"Who would've thought a bit of musty old muslin could make one feel so… strange," she murmured before the ghost moved out of her path.

"It's not just the costume…" Charlie began, "it's…"

"All the memories of times gone by," she continued absent-mindedly. "Will you excuse me while I check the cellar?"

Once the two men were alone, Charlie noticed the ghost seemed just as affected by his recent encounter as the girl had been. Even more so, perhaps, but he quickly reverted to type.

"They say places always look smaller than you remember them, but this kitchen seems huge to me now."

"You could use it to cater for an army," agreed Charlie, looking at the range.

"Exactly what I was thinking."

The radio repairman was just reflecting on how odd it

was that they should both agree on something when Fiona returned. "This is terribly embarrassing, but I can't seem to find the key."

"Punch will be fine," said Charlie and meant it.

"For you, perhaps," she continued with a laugh, "but I'm afraid others won't be so good-natured about it." And with that she led them back in the direction from which they had come.

Swirling dancers filled the floor whilst other guests were grazing along the trestle tables that lined one side of the room. Fiona steered Charlie towards the punch bowl where Angus was ladling out the concoction.

"There's food too, so do tuck in."

Whilst Angus was filling his glass, Charlie allowed his eyes to further explore his surroundings. If the kitchen was a hall and the hall was a house, then the hall at his house was no hall at all. Everything was larger than life, but then life wasn't a pantomime, or was it? He looked round for the girl but she seemed to have vanished. Only the rippling of the tablecloth near his feet suggested a clue as to her whereabouts. Bending down to lift the cloth he found her crawling on her hands and knees.

"Shortcut," she smiled by way of explanation before gesturing for him to let the cloth down again. He stood up and tried to look relaxed, but the effort only made him feel more self-conscious than ever. Meanwhile, beneath the table, Fiona had discovered the scruffy boys squatting on a cross support and guarding several bottles of whisky. Giving them a conspiratorial wink in passing, she emerged on the other side and stood to whisper to Angus. Charlie couldn't make out a word, but whatever the gen, it didn't seem to surprise the man with the ladle very much. No sooner had she finished imparting her information than the pair of them began scanning the room. Having nothing better to do, Charlie decided to do the same.

His attention was soon drawn to one of the trestle tables where Caird was making the most of his single ghostly power. Thankfully, so far, no one else seemed to have noticed the way the cheese sandwiches appeared to levitate before vanishing into thin air, or into the heavy heir, depending on your point of view. Charlie, of course, got the whole picture, but to his alarm he soon realised that the two children standing nearby did not. He was just about to intervene when Fiona reappeared at his side.

"Look, Miss..." he began, as he watched Cameron and Martha run over to their mother and tug at her apron strings.

"Fiona, please," she insisted, mistaking his awkwardness for excess formality.

Amy, despite being rushed off her feet, also glanced over to where her children were pointing and quickly wished she hadn't for, at that precise moment, a mince pie vanished before her eyes. Charlie waited for the commotion that he knew would follow. It might be large, it might be small, but it would come, and it would distract this mercurial girl's attention and complicate his task still further. Then Amy dropped her tray. It could have been worse, she might have screamed, but Fiona was already moving away. "I have to talk to you," he called after her, "on a matter of grave..." Surely there was a less unfortunate word than that? As he tried to rephrase, he noticed the

78

woman in the apron run up to the man serving punch. "…
of pressing importance," he resumed more forcefully.

"Trust me, few things are more pressing then a Scot
without a dram on Hogmanay," Fiona answered with a
departing smile.

His eyes tracked her across the room and over to Ivan,
who had just entered with Lady Caird on his arm. Sighing,
Charlie returned his attention to the pair just across the
table. The maid's words were too fast and too low for him
to hear, but Angus's were not.

"Tsh! And what's a castle without one?" he was saying.
"Surely you wouldn't want the shame of living in a second-
rate establishment?"

The teasing did little to soothe the housekeeper and she
left without further comment, but it made the repairman
feel calmer. Once she had gone, the man with the ladle
actually grinned at him, "Top up your glass, sir?"

He was just taking a grateful sip when the ghost
ambled over to his side.

"Cousin Ivan's being his usual happy self by the look
of it."

Charlie noticed that Lady Caird had begun to circulate
around the room leaving the little man glowering by the
door. It was then that he became doubly grateful for his
refill, for the glass would help disguise his lip movements
and just might, possibly, avert the impression he was
talking to himself. Even so, it would probably be a good
idea to steer the ghost somewhere a little less conspicuous.
Approaching a likely looking corner, Charlie raised the
tumbler to his lips. "He wasn't exactly welcoming when
we arrived," he acknowledged.

"Probably afraid everyone's drinking away his inheritance."

"*His* inheritance?" queried Charlie.

"In the absence of a will and as the next male in line, the estate passes to him."

"What about Fiona?"

"As I never made an honest woman of her, she has no legal claim."

"That's vexing, and no mistake."

The ghost frowned and glanced back at Ivan. "It is, and so's he."

On the other side of the room, Ivan was living up to his reputation by having another heated exchange with the Land Girl. As they were near the door, guests were coming and going throughout, and each time someone passed, the bickering pair were forced to lower their voices, which required ever increasing amounts of self-control. Of the two, Fiona seemed closer to her limit.

"As hostess I rather think I should be the judge of what's served in this house."

"After witnessing tonight's free-for-all I doubt your ability to be the judge of anything."

"Charles and I both understood the need to move with the times."

"The man's dead!"

"*Missing, presumed dead,*" corrected Fiona, "and until seven years has elapsed, he remains missing."

"Dead."

By now they were both speaking over each other, but at least Ivan had deigned to look at her.

"Why don't you just accept it? That deluded laird of

yours is never going to return waving wills and marriage certificates under your nose."

"And how typical of you to put paperwork above all else. But then, you're a civil servant, aren't you!"

"Charles mentioned my work for the ministry?"

"Oh yes, I heard all about The Foolscap Fusiliers."[14]

Ivan's eyes narrowed.

Fortunately, Amy returned at that moment clutching a dustpan and brush, which she waved aloft for them to see.

"Found them," she said triumphantly before registering Ivan's glare and shrinking back to her usual diminutive self again. Instinctively, Fiona placed an arm around the housekeeper's shoulders and escorted her away to safety.

Whilst Amy got to work sweeping up the pieces of broken plate, Fiona had reclaimed her basket and started lobbing oranges at various members of the band. This seemed to go some way to restoring the party mood, both for them and her. The ghost tapped his watch and Charlie nodded. He was only too aware how time was ticking and was just about to say so when Fiona grabbed his arm.

"Now, let's see how good you are at talking and dancing at the same time," she said with a mischievous grin.

Before he could protest, she had pulled him onto the centre of the floor and given a signal for the bandleader to play something energetic. As guests began to crowd around them any hopes Charlie may have had of having a quiet word were dashed, and it took all his concentration just trying to follow the twists and turns of the other dancers.

---

14   A widely used size of paper during the period which originally got its name from a watermark featuring a fool's cap and bells. It remains the standard size for legal documents within the U.S.A.

Villagers were waving French flags, dancing to the music of an accordion, and doing their best to encourage a small unit of British soldiers to join in with their festivities. Charles Caird, who was leading the unit, took a swig from one of the wine bottles being offered plus a large chunk of bread. Others had to endure having flowers put in their helmets, which they did with good grace. Amongst their group was a Radio Operator carrying a small portable radio set and, bringing up the rear, were Charlie and Saunders toting the larger W.S. 18 model.

Suddenly, there was a burst of gunfire. Everybody ducked and, whilst the villagers ran to take cover indoors, the radio operator pointed to a lone sniper in a grey uniform retreating across a field some distance away. Caird beckoned his men off in pursuit but instructed Charlie and Saunders to remain behind. Left alone, the two men wasted no time in getting their set operational before waiting and watching.

After a short while an old innkeeper called down to Saunders from a bedroom window. Saunders looked up and saw the man beckoning him inside. The man indicated that Saunders would get a better lookout if he joined him at the upstairs window. Saunders tapped Charlie on the shoulder, gesturing where he was going. Charlie nodded whilst listening for anything coming through the headphones.

*

"Mind where you're going, you idiot!" said an unidentified male voice.

Dizzy and disorientated, it took Charlie a second to realise that his shoe buckle had caught in the hem of a dancer's long skirt and that an ever-lengthening strip was starting to unravel away from it. Attempting to bend down and undo the trip hazard, he was jostled and bumped so much that he was forced to keep moving. However, it scarcely took another second before people did indeed start tripping and falling all around him. Standing aloof, Ivan had been well placed to spot the problem and moving over to the side of the dance floor he gave the rag rope a tug. Unfortunately, the tug came just as Charlie managed to unhitch the tartan tangle from his shoe. With all the tension gone from the other end, Ivan, who was still pulling hard, stumbled backwards onto a table. The pratfall was greeted by roars of laughter and loud whistles from around the room.

Charlie ran over to assist, but Ivan's look was so fierce he stopped in his tracks. All he could do was watch breathlessly as the dishevelled man got to his feet, removed a sausage roll from his pocket and squeezed it to a pulp with his fist. Taking the hint, Charlie stumbled away onto the terrace outside and was quickly followed by Fiona.

Amy, meanwhile, had also appeared from the beneath the wreckage and, taking in the full scale of the damage, turned to Angus. "I think I'll be fetching a bigger brush," she sighed.

Chapter Seventeen

CHARLIE LURCHED FOR THE BALUSTRADE WHILST Fiona skipped along behind. Catching up with him she tossed her basket in the air, did a quick spin, and caught it again before collapsing in laughter.

"Oh I needed that," she exclaimed with feeling.

"I should… go back… and apologise," gasped the repairman.

"To Ivan? Don't you dare! He could do with being taken down a peg or two, believe me."

They both peered inside where they could see the dancers continuing their reel and the man himself glaring out at them.

"What was it you wanted to tell me?"

As Charlie could still only gasp in reply, she turned the basket upside down and tried it on for a hat. "A minute – please," he begged.

"A whole one?"

He nodded and proffered his wristwatch for her to see.

But, with seventeenth-century shirts being a whole lot more voluminous than their modern equivalents, she ended up having to hold his wrist quite firmly in order to push back all the folds of material and locate the timepiece beneath. He'd forgotten what it felt like to be held by such a pretty girl, any girl for that matter, and the sensation of her touch came as a surprise to him.

"My, your pulse really is racing, isn't it?" she announced once the minute was up.

Damn. He'd held her gaze too long and knew it.

"I should check that the fireworks are ready," she said, letting his wrist fall.

"Blast the fireworks!"

"That's the intention all right."

"Some people just carry a lump of coal through the house."

"Do they? How fascinating. We must compare notes when I get back. You will still be here when I get back, won't you?" She was already moving away.

"In for a penny in for a pound."

"Are you always so droll?" she asked, smiling her *hello and goodbye* smile.

"I don't know, I can't remember," Charlie called back, and he really couldn't.

He wondered at the speed with which the white of her blouse was absorbed into the darkness and suddenly felt very alone. He'd forgotten that feeling too. Although solitude had been his preferred state ever since he'd been invalided out of the army, he had never felt self-conscious about it. Not until then, that is. How many more things had he forgotten about? He had been trying to remember something that morning, hadn't he? What was it again? It began with a letter. And as he wandered along the terrace looking for another way into the building, he could be heard muttering to himself, "W, w, w."

Still dishevelled, Ivan burst into the library, went over to the drinks cabinet and poured himself a large measure. After a couple of restorative gulps, he became less agitated and his eye settled on the decanter he'd just used. It wasn't at the proper angle and it bothered him. Things that didn't square with his way of thinking always did. So, he readjusted it until it was just so before carrying his glass over to the desk and picking up the phone.

"Hello, put me through to the police," he ordered.

While he was waiting to be connected, he glanced up at the portrait of Charles Caird that hung above the fireplace. Then the receiver crackled.

"And about time too," he snapped. "Listen, this is Castle Caird and we seem to have an unruly element here tonight that's threatening to get out of hand."

Just then there was a knock on the door and, not getting any reply from inside, the handle turned.

"I don't care about that," the caller continued, now more hushed than before. "You just get someone up here and tell them that the ringleader is wearing a pantomime costume." There was another short pause during which Ivan evidently forgot his temporary caution, "No, I don't know which pantomime character!" Having slammed the phone down he looked up and saw Finlay.

"Ah, the family solicitor enters. No need to ask whose side you're on in all this?"

"I always try to be equitable," the old man replied calmly.

Ivan merely snorted.

"But such impatience on your part. Why not let legal process take its course?" asked the old man as he took a couple of steps further into the room.

"And in the meantime?" asked Ivan getting up to block any further advance. "Open your eyes, man, the place is being run by a complete cracker box of characters."

Finlay, for his part, read Ivan's tactics well enough but bought extra time by brushing a stray party streamer from his jacket.

"I've always been rather fond of crackers myself," he replied with a smile, "and not just the ones you find on the table at Christmas, either. Perhaps it's discovering the surprise inside."

"Just a lot of silly hats and nonsense," huffed the little man. He wanted to escort Finlay to the door but, even steering him by the elbow, the old man seemed a lot slower retreating than he was at advancing.

"Ah yes, the humour and the hat swapping," the solicitor continued. "Both have proved rather essential over the last few years, haven't they? What with city girls answering the call to work on the land and liking it, former army catering corps personnel finding it in them to become chefs, and women who might otherwise have remained housewives…"

"… Should now go home and take their filthy children with them."

Ivan made an effort to regain his composure again.

"Surely you can see that the business of running things should – *no, must* – be left to people who were born to do it?"

Even with his deliberately slowed pace, Finlay found

they had now reached the door but he held Ivan in his gaze a moment longer. "The irony being, of course, that sometimes those people are the least adaptable and most humourless of all."

This was the last straw for Ivan and his fragile self-control collapsed completely.

"You can tell your clients that I shall be making an announcement at midnight." He made it sound as much of a threat as a promise.

"In that case," said Finlay, finally flashing the steel himself, "you could do a lot worse than remember something I read as a student, not in a cracker admittedly, but still relevant: the word *communication* from the Latin *communus*, being a noun that meant community or sharing. Now, if you'll excuse me."

And Ivan was happy to do so.

Once the door was closed again, he returned to the desk and this was his position of choice. Checking figures. Following procedures. Ordered. Working in Whitehall had certainly cushioned him during the war. True, he had to endure the air raids, the flying bombs and all the other trials and tribulations of living in the capital, but as a civil servant, he *himself* had not had to change fundamentally. His social circle had remained the same, albeit depleted in numbers. For the most part he had continued to frequent the same clubs, restaurants and drawing rooms as before. Continuity and maintaining his way of life had not only been a personal choice but a patriotic one. At least that's the way he saw it. But now all some people wanted was to upset the apple cart. Or was it an orange cart?

Chapter Eighteen

CHARLIE HAD RE-ENTERED THE CASTLE BY THE main entrance hall, which was now empty. Empty apart from Amy, who was trying to wrestle a broom from a cupboard. It seemed like the fishing rods and other paraphernalia stored there were about to tumble out and engulf her. Charlie hurried over and held back the clutter while the woman finally managed to pull her broom free. Then, together, they performed a nifty shuffle in which he used all his might to hold the door closed whilst she fastened the latch.

"You have to watch out for the white elephants," she gasped.

Charlie smiled back before noticing Charles Caird sitting on the stairs above them.

"Only one thing to do," he replied as much to himself as to her.

"What's that?"

"Walk up and look them straight in the eye."

"I'll try and remember that," she said.

"Me too," said Charlie as he turned and began climbing the stairs.

"Any progress?" asked the ghost whilst Charlie was still several steps below.

Charlie shook his head. "I feel like a total imposter."

"Well, if it's any consolation, so do I," replied the ghost.

"But these are your people."

"But *I* can't reach out and touch them, can I? *I* can't reach out and *I* sure as hell can't dance with my girl the way *you* just did."

"I was only trying to hold her attention," protested Charlie, feeling very self-conscious again.

"Oh, you were doing that all right," blazed Caird. But just as the scrutiny was getting too much, it was the ghost who looked away. "Maybe she's forgotten me already," he added almost as an afterthought.

"Rubbish!" retorted Charlie, surprising himself with the force of his reply. Was he protesting too much? "Didn't you see the way she looked when you tried to kiss her in the kitchen?"

"It's natural to wonder, though, isn't it? continued the ghost, warming to his theme. "A pretty woman like her. Don't you ever wonder about your wife?"

Charlie wondered about her for a moment, the first moment in a long while.

W, w, w. Was w for "wife", he wondered? No. "She's definitely an ex now, I think," he said eventually.

Suddenly the ghost was up and away so fast that Charlie had to hurry to catch up.

"Where are we going now?"

"I just want to see if she kept my letters," said Caird without looking round.

"Jealousy and suspicion are like ugly sisters," replied Charlie, alarmed by the apparent detour.

"Then they should feel right at home, shouldn't they?" retorted the ghost, taking two steps at a time.

"They belong in a Victorian novel."

"Why not a pantomime too?"

"Because *Wuthering Tights* would have too many wrinkles," gasped Charlie as he rounded a corner and almost ran into the ghost's outstretched arm.

They were now at the start of a corridor and the ghost had just noticed Ivan disappearing down the far end of it. As soon as the coast was clear he beckoned the repairman on again.

"And what's a few wrinkles here and there?"

"A few too many, especially if I'm the one that has to iron them out afterwards," answered Charlie as they stopped outside the door to the library.

"No ironing required, just a little light handle turning," said the ghost.

Charlie let them both in. "I meant what I said," he persisted once they were inside. "This is getting far too personal for me."

"So's my will, and you're a party to that, aren't you? Besides, do I really seem like the soppy letter sort?"

"No, I suppose not," admitted Charlie.

"No, of course not," huffed the ghost as he moved towards a desk. "Here, just see if you can get this open, will you?"

Charlie tried to open the desk and to his great relief found that it was locked. "Let's just leave it, shall we?"

"You can use the letter opener to pick the lock."

"That's breaking and entering."

"You forget, I've seen you using a screwdriver. Very nimble. All in the wrist, no doubt."

Charlie forced himself to count to ten before setting to work and, annoyingly, managed to spring the latch almost immediately.

"There they are, with the string around them," cried Caird as soon as the lid was open.

"Satisfied now?" asked Charlie, eager to get the thing closed up again as fast as possible.

The ghost, however, was not satisfied and directed his accomplice to retrieve an assortment of letters and notebooks and seat himself down on a chair. Groaning inwardly, Charlie did as he was directed but, as he began sifting through the collection, his attitude began to change. He glanced up at Caird, trying to reconcile the face which was peering over his shoulder with the author of the work he held in his hands.

"I'd never have taken you for a diarist, though."

"Just jottings," the ghost answered modestly. "But I'd listen to the way chaps would talk about how they wanted things after the war was all over – fairer opportunities – better health care – a decent roof over one's head…"

"That's Aladdin's three wishes right there," said Charlie, more impressed than ever.

"Quite so, and it set me thinking about how to implement some changes. Up here on the estate, I mean. Only I hadn't found the big puff of smoke and whoosh thing where it all comes together."

There was an awkward pause while he examined the holes in his tunic. "Seems like the whoosh found me first."

"I see," murmured Charlie, only to be startled by an angry voice on the other side of the room.

"See what, exactly?" Fiona demanded.

In his confusion, Charlie stood up so suddenly that all the papers fell from his lap onto the carpet. He looked to the ghost for assistance but all Caird could do was make "keep calm" gestures with his hands.

"Don't shoot, I'm only the messenger," pleaded Charlie, raising his arms in surrender.

"Thief, more like," said the girl.

"No. You've got the wrong end of the stick entirely. I was only..."

As he bent down to pick up the papers, she grabbed the poker from the fireplace and began wielding it threateningly. "You must leave those where they are. They're the most precious things I've got left and you've violated them enough already."

He was in no doubt that she intended to take a swipe at him, but as he tried to back out of range, he tripped over the chair he'd been sitting on.

"Come on, out! Or would you rather I called the dogs?"

In desperation Charlie glanced at Caird again but the ghost seemed just as calm as before.

"That's not a bad idea, come to think of it," was all he said.

"What?" Charlie asked incredulously.

"I was talking to Fiona," said the ghost.

"Didn't your experience on the phone tell you anything?" Charlie expostulated.

"Not enough obviously," replied Fiona, naturally assuming Charlie was talking to her.

"Sorry, force of habit," said the ghost with a look of adoration on his face, "and she is looking particularly stunning tonight."

Deciding it was pointless seeking any further practical assistance from that quarter, Charlie directed his attention back to the Land Girl. "I did try to explain earlier, honestly I did."

"It's true, he did you know," the ghost seconded.

"Hollow words, Mr Goodman, hollow words. I bet that isn't even your real name either, is it?"

"No, I mean, yes," stammered Charlie defensively. Things were getting complicated.

"Now if you'd just hear me out about the dogs," the ghost was saying, but to whom?

Charlie pointed a questioning finger first to himself and then to Fiona, then the ghost pointed at Charlie.

"Have you taken leave of your senses?" Charlie asked him.

"Curious as it may seem, I think I'm just coming to them," interjected Fiona.

"Man's best friend, remember," continued the ghost to Charlie.

"Who are you talking to now?" the radio repairman asked at a loss.

"*You!*" the other two shouted together.

Charlie buried his head in his hands before peering out at Caird. It looked as if the ghost was blatantly mocking him now by lifting a hand to each temple and waving his fingers at him. "Think ears man. Ears!" he was saying and even though the tone was serious, the gestures certainly were not.

Well, that's gratitude for you, thought Charlie. *Try and help a person and they make out you're nothing but an ass.* And then the girl was speaking too, "You really leave me no alternative," she was saying.

Then, cupping her hands to her mouth, she whistled towards the doorway.

"Oh good, now I'm in *The Hound of the Baskervilles*," said Charlie to no one in particular.

No sooner had he spoken than two Irish wolfhounds bounded into the room.

"Two hounds. Plural. Even better," he groaned as the dogs edged toward him, their hackles rising.

"Well, don't just stand there, say something," he beseeched the ghost.

"Oh no, I'm not going to call them off, if that's what you think," said Fiona, her voice colder than ever.

"Not you, *him!*" quavered Charlie, his voice raised to its highest pitch. He inclined his head in the ghost's direction and the dogs began to bark in unison.

Suddenly there was another whistle and in a commanding voice the ghost called, "Horace! Hector!"

The dog's ears twitched and, just as suddenly, they fell silent.

"Now lie down. *Lie*," ordered Caird.

Turning to where Charles was standing both dogs sniffed the air and lay down obediently.

"Pulse rate any better now?" the ghost asked Charlie with a wicked leer.

Charlie nodded and let out an enormous sigh of relief while Fiona scrutinised him, curiosity starting to get the better of her anger. "How did you do that?" she asked.

"I didn't do anything," he replied before turning to the ghost. "It was their master's voice they responded to. Their hearing's a whole lot more acute than ours, you see."

The ghost slapped his head, "Finally," he said in exasperation.

"Charles? Are you trying to tell me that Charles is here?" the Land Girl asked, her defences lowering ever so slightly.

"In a manner of speaking," Charlie replied, as he tried to assess the range of the poker, even though he was now almost too exhausted to care what she did with it. "Marconi had a theory that sound waves never end, they just get weaker and weaker the further they travel."

The girl's eyes moved over to the fireplace. "My irrational outbursts," she murmured.

"They have to go somewhere, don't they?" Charlie continued gently.

"I don't know. I was never very hot on the sciences."

"Well, either way, he just wants you to know that he did make a will after all."

Suddenly the poker was raised again and she was waving it at him while her mind tried to process this latest bit of information.

"Now don't go rushing your fences, fancy breeches," she warned.

"I have no choice," said Charlie, bravely trying to hold his ground and concentrating very hard. "In wartime, when a soldier is close to death, he can make a verbal will – and it's valid – if there are two witnesses present and…" He stopped suddenly and turned to the ghost. "That's it!" he said, "W is for witness!"

"So by my reckoning that makes you one witness short of a hoax doesn't it, Mr… ?"

"Yes. No. *No!*" Charlie shot back as he punched his knee several times in frustration. "Not if you have a transcript, and I do, right here, right in my…" He reached into his jacket pocket and realised yet another horrible mistake. "The notebook – in my other jacket – which I left in the van."

That was when she lunged at him and he was forced to scramble around the room until he was by the bookshelves. He ducked and weaved until he could get his hands on a volume of the *Encyclopaedia Britannica*, which he then used as a shield against her blows. The dogs were growling again by this point and started to close in, until Caird whistled for them to stop. Sensing this was his last opportunity to take defensive action, Charlie did the only thing his brain could come up with, and that was to busk it. "The *Encyclopaedia Britannica* is meant to have an entry about everything, right?" he began uncertainly as tried to remember the sales pitch deployed by a salesman who used to flog the things on HP before the war.

"I never put it to the test," said Fiona.

"So why not give it a go today?" replied Charlie in what he hoped was his best sales voice.

"Here, even if you don't believe the bit about me and the second witness, you can still check up on the entry about verbal wills, can't you? Go on, Wills – verbal."

As she took the book, he held up both hands again – the second signal of surrender that evening. The only difference being that this time the forefingers of each hand were visibly and most firmly crossed.

"And if you're not entirely satisfied, there's no obligation to buy the whole set and we'll return your deposit to you," he concluded backing away again, which wasn't a good idea because he backed into a chair and fell into it. As the girl started reading, the repairman looked up at the ghost who indicated the time on his watch.

"*Verbal will, otherwise known as* nuncupative, *that must have two witnesses and only deal in the distribution of property.*" It was then her turn to look up, and while she did all three heard the door being locked from the outside.

Chapter Nineteen

IVAN REMOVED THE KEY, REGARDED IT LIKE AN OLD friend and slipped it into a pocket. If that seems like an extreme reaction to an awkward situation, it is important to remember that Ivan, who had been working in various government departments for many years, had come to believe that certain office practices could be applied outside of it as well. Unlike Lady Caird, he had found that problems really did seem to vanish if locked away. Bigger problems just required bigger filing cabinets, that was all. By the time said problem had been rediscovered, you had hopefully been promoted upwards to another department. Fiona, never having been a civil servant herself, ran to the door, rattled the handle and yelled Ivan's name through the keyhole.

This was annoying to Ivan. He had put the problem in the metaphorical *pending* folder and now someone was making a noise about it, far too much noise. What's more, there was a phone line running out of the library and along the wainscoting close to where he was standing. This meant they could, at any moment, start making a noise to someone else too. This annoyed him even more because, if there is one thing a bureaucrat dislikes more than having their judgment questioned, it is the idea of people going behind their backs and getting satisfaction elsewhere. Allow that to happen and next thing you knew there'd be anarchy on the streets! He therefore felt he had no choice but to yank the telephone cable away from its fixtures. "It's always been two against one with you, hasn't it, Fiona?" he huffed whilst tugging the wire. Once the cable was loose, he set about cutting it with the sharp edge of the key. "First you and Charles gang up on me, and now he's gone you've roped in this pantomime prince as a stand-in."

Back on her side of the door Fiona was ready to fight back, "Why would we gang up on you when we hardly ever saw you? You only came running back here once you thought your way was clear to the title."

The ghost evidently thought she'd bowled a winner with this one and mimed batting a cricket ball into the distance.

"And as for Mr Goodman here, he's in radio and we were just discussing a conjuring trick he hopes to perform later tonight."

The ghost liked that reply too but Charlie definitely didn't and started to shake his head vigorously.

Ivan's response through the woodwork only made matters worse. "So now we've got a magician who works in radio! Well, that confirms something at least."

"Confirms what?" snapped Fiona.

"What you said a few minutes ago about being irrational." Ivan was back in charge now and enjoying it.

Fiona kicked the door in frustration, "And as for those who stoop to listen through keyholes…"

While this had been going on, Charlie had picked up the letter opener again and, once she had stopped assaulting the door, he squeezed past and tried to force the lock. For a moment it looked like he might manage the trick twice in a row, then the blade snapped.

"Try the phone," suggested the girl.

Charlie ran back to the desk and lifted the receiver before glancing back at her in shock.

"The line's gone dead!" he said, blanched of all colour.

"Too late." Fiona sighed before slapping the door one last time with the palm of her hand.

"Why do people have to keep saying that?" asked Charlie in an anguished voice.

1944

As soon as Saunders had entered the inn, several women pointed him up the stairs. Looking into a room leading off the landing he saw the innkeeper standing to one side of the window, so he ran over to take up position on the other. Removing his field glasses he scanned the horizon whilst making sure he remained obscured by the curtain. Panning and adjusting his focus at the same time, he spotted the lone sniper rejoining a group of similarly uniformed troops as they beat a hasty retreat along a hedge. Saunders then panned back and saw Caird's troops running along a sunken lane.

Saunders watched in alarm as both sets of troops began to draw parallel, even though they were effectively screened from each other by the hedge and the depression of the lane. Then Caird's men actually drew in front, the pursuers overtaking the pursued, at which point Saunders

called down to Charlie outside. Charlie immediately
started relaying what Saunders was telling him into the
voice piece, but before he had a chance to finish, something
he heard through the earphones made him flinch.

*

Marge rearranged the rug over the four sleeping children in the back of the car before pulling another one up over herself. Then she peered through the darkness of the pub car park in time to see Saunders running towards them. Even with the rug up to her chin she shivered as the door opened, letting in an icy gust of wind.

"The local station has just logged a call from a place called Caird Castle. It was to report a potential disturbance of the peace."

"Charlie wouldn't say *boo* to a goose. Least ways not anymore!" Marge replied between chattering teeth.

"They say the man concerned is wearing a pantomime costume."

"But surely you don't think…"

"Uncle Charlie took us to the pantomime," came a sleepy voice from the back seat.

Both adults swivelled round as Albert blinked back at them drowsily.

"Oh, Lor…"

"Luckily, they're too short-staffed to send anyone up there at the moment," Saunders continued. "So, I said I'd go."

"And luckily you're someone who understands," Marge added with feeling.

The cop glanced at his watch and started the engine.

"A couple of inches either way and it could have been me that took that hit to the head, not Charlie. What then, would people be reporting me for being a nuisance too?"

*

A few miles further north Charlie was also getting chilled to the marrow and standing spreadeagled against a castle wall wasn't helping. Fiona was waiting impatiently inside a window to his right, whilst the two dogs were leaning out of the window on his left, growling. Unwisely, he had just taken a peek over the ledge on which he was perched and had recoiled instantly. His back was now so hard against the stonework that he was certain he could feel chisel marks through his clothes. It took several lungfuls of cold night air before he could force himself onwards again. One step, then another, before falling past her into the room.

She wasted no time on sympathy, merely closing the window whilst he picked himself up off the floor.

"All present and correct?"

Charlie checked himself for injuries and then looked up to see the ghost leaning against the door frame. He nodded at her.

"I'll take that as a yes then," she replied before running over to a dumbwaiter set in the wall.[15]

After tugging on the rope the platform arrived in the opening and she climbed in.

---

15   A small elevator or lift used to carry food which, at the time of our story, would have been operated by a rope pully mechanism.

"What's wrong with the door?" Charlie asked.

"No danger of bumping into Ivan this way. I'll send it straight up again."

He watched her descend and then turned to the ghost.

"How did you get in here before us?"

"I used the door like any normal person," Caird replied.

"But you can't handle door handles," protested Charlie.

"I may not be able to open or close them, but that doesn't mean I can't pass through them. One has to be precise with language, remember?"

Charlie pondered on how being ribbed by a ghost always had one at a disadvantage. He was still pondering when the contraption appeared in the hatchway again.

"Get in, you Yorkshire Pudding," encouraged the ghost, so he went over and folded himself inside.

If you can't stand the heat, get out of the kitchen, was Charlie's first thought once he had extricated himself at the other end. Fiona had just sent the contraption up again to collect the ghost and he was face to face with Angus and Fergus again. Only now that the twins were both backstage, as it were, they had divested themselves of their jackets and rolled up their sleeves.

"Persuade Angus and Fergus and you'll have persuaded me," said the girl while looking at the kitchen clock. "And don't take too long, rumour has it there's another act waiting in the wings."

Charlie glanced from the girl back to the duo. As they folded their arms in true *Okay, show us what you've got* fashion, he noted the assortment of military tattoos on display.

"They look like a tough crowd," he murmured.

Realising that intimidation may not be the best tactic, Angus dropped his pose, picked up a glass and began wiping it. "Do you perform for a living?" he asked lightly.

"No, only the dead," stammered Charlie as the dumbwaiter returned and the ghost got out. Although it had been a tight squeeze, the temptation to revisit a childhood pastime had probably been too much for him to resist.

"And here he is now!" resumed the repairman in his nervous salesman voice.

Angus and Fergus both glanced at the empty hatchway and then back at Charlie.

"Who's he then, the Invisible Man?" asked Angus.

"The Invisible Man had bandages and a pair of sunglasses" corrected Fergus. "Did you not catch that picture with Claude Raines?"

"Aye, I saw *that* all right," Angus replied before turning back to Charlie. "You'll never top the bill at the Empire, laddie," he said before turning to pick up another glass. But this time, just as he started to use a cloth on it, the glass began to squeak and it gave Charlie an idea. Looking round the room his eyes settled on a yard of ale glass hanging on the wall.[16] He then grabbed a chair and placed it underneath the bulb end.

"If the lady would care to climb up and rest her ear against the end of this glass receptacle?"

And Fiona, being the kind of girl she was, immediately did.

---

16 A glass approximately 1 yard (90cm) long that holds two and a half pints of beer. It has a bulb at one end rising up a long shaft to form an open fluted end at the other. Thought to have originated in England in the seventeenth century.

Charlie beckoned the twins to come closer before he placed a second chair for the ghost to stand on and talk into the fluted end. As the ghost climbed up, the others noticed how the chair started to wobble and Charlie continued his build-up.

"She will then shortly hear Charles Caird blowing his own trumpet – a feat for which he is widely renowned."

The ghost took a deep breath and then whistled, very high and shrill, alternating between two notes like a bosun's signal.

Fiona pressed her ear closer to the glass and began to smile. "I can feel something!"

"He's whistling," explained Charlie.

"Is that what he did with the dogs?"

"No, he spoke to them as well."

"How typical," she said with mock annoyance. "He thinks more of those old mutts than he does of me. What does *Hello* feel like, I wonder?"

"Hello," bellowed the ghost.

Her face lit up. "Yes. And Fiona?"

"F-I-O-N-A!" came the reply.

"It was strongest before the end," said the recipient, slightly disappointed this time.

"A consonant."

"Oh."

Angus and Fergus drew closer still and also rested their ears on the tube.

"Remember the family motto," said the ghost.

Fiona shook her head at Charlie, "Barely anything that time either."

"Remember the family motto," repeated Charlie.

"We see it through," she exclaimed excitedly, as much to her interpreter as to the ghost.

"I will, I will, I promise," she continued returning her attention to the far end of the glass again.

"Look, condensation!" Angus said, turning to his brother. The ghost had noticed it too and, wiping the moisture from the rim of the glass with his fingers, created a ringing tone. At this point Angus went back to the table and picked up the glass he had been drying.

"Love to you and the old girl," the ghost continued to Fiona.

The Land Girl turned to Charlie again, "You'll have to decipher," it was a request as much as an instruction.

"He sends his love to you and his mother," said Charlie, slightly embarrassed by the personal nature of the message.

"And we return it – a hundredfold, more…" she bit her lip as emotion welled up inside. "What's happening now?"

"He's whistling again – I think that means he's signing off."

"Away with his whistling," interrupted Angus. "Tell him to wipe instead."

The ghost did as he was directed and when the ringing tone was made, Angus used the glass he was holding to make a tone that harmonised with it. The others then followed his lead by picking up any glass items they could lay their hands on. Within seconds they were performing a surprisingly jaunty little tune. So jaunty in fact that no one heard Ivan enter.

"Well, well, well. Some people just don't know what's good for them, do they?" he sneered.

"Truth will out," replied Angus, who was first to recover from the interruption.

"Truth! Is that what you call this hocus pocus?" And with that he picked up a pan and threw it at the neck of the yard glass, which shattered instantly.

Angus stepped in front of the intruder. "You need to calm down some," said the chef.

At that moment Charlie suddenly staggered and Fiona hopped down from her chair and ran over to him. "You're bleeding."

The change from jollity to violence had been so sudden that it made the sight all the more shocking.

"Help me with him, will you?" she said turning to Fergus.

Fergus was just moving over to assist when the cold voice rang out again. "Leave him where he is, that man has been reported to the police."

"Police!" exclaimed the ghost.

Ivan tried to get at Charlie, but again Angus blocked the way before directing his brother to shepherd the injured man out through the door to the right of the oven range.

Fergus and Charlie reached the door and then, just before it closed behind them, the ghost slipped through too. Once they were safely on the other side, the latch was locked and Fergus held up the key. "You can't win 'em all, pal, you can't win 'em all," he taunted through the windowpane.

At this Ivan rushed past the chef and tried the handle.

"Now you can see how much you like it," said Fiona watching the tantrum. Ivan spun round, unsure who to tackle next.

"You run along, Miss. You can leave Mr Ivan to me," said Angus.

Picking her moment, Fiona managed to skirt past Ivan and up the stairs, leaving the two men to battle it out alone.

The battle began as a crab dance. When Angus moved sideways along one end of the table to block Ivan, Ivan moved sideways in the same direction at the other end, to block Angus. The back and forth went on for several seconds until Ivan picked up the table and turned it over.

This would have been an extreme provocation for anyone with an ounce of pride in the culinary arts, but Angus had a whole lot more than that.

"Mess up my kitchen would you, you wee bastard?" he shouted as he leaped over the mess.

He was about to lay hold of Ivan when the smaller man grabbed a pepper pot off the floor and threw the contents into the Scotsman's face.

"It's *my* kitchen by rights *and* all the rest besides," hissed Ivan as Angus covered his eyes in pain.

"Your rights!" sneezed Angus in disgust.

Despite his discomfort, the chef tried to trip Ivan before he could leave to follow Fiona. But it only worked as a temporary stall, after which he had to stagger to the sink to bathe his streaming eyes. Ivan then took his chance and ran after the girl, almost knocking Amy and her tray over in the process.

Once her balance was recovered, Amy looked down at what she was carrying, selected a large ball of haggis and lobbed it straight at the back of Ivan's head. Not only was it a direct hit but, even more satisfyingly, it broke on impact and stuck to the man's hair. She then ran over to assist her husband.

Chapter Twenty

THE GHOST WAS LEANING OVER CHARLIE AS HE attempted to push the van out of the stable.

Solid coach work was all very well but it didn't make for light pushing, that was for sure.

He was grateful when Fergus had opened the doors and come back to lend a hand.

The footman was certainly observant, Charlie decided. He'd even read the paint work on the side vehicle before leaning into it with his shoulder.

"Come on, we've only got fifteen minutes left," urged the ghost.

Charlie looked up at him, the gash on his forehead still visible in the gloom, and when he spoke his voice was groggy.

"If you hadn't put sugar in the petrol tank, we wouldn't need to be pushing this thing in the first place, would we?"

"You were about to go AWOL, dammit," the ghost shot back.

"Sugar in the engine? That sounds like the Laird all right. A fine pair for pranks, he and Miss Fiona both," smiled Fergus, recalling happier days.

"You don't say."

"But never anything really nasty, mind," the footman continued. "I reckon we all saw enough of the nasty stuff while we were in the services."

It was now Charlie's turn to be reflective. "I noticed the military tattoos," he replied.

Fergus tapped his head, "I only wish some of the pictures up here would fade as fast."

Charlie shook his own head and then wished he hadn't. It hurt enough already and the idea that a man who wanted to forget was now helping a man who needed to remember made it pound even more. It was too much to process just then so he bent down and concentrated on pushing.

"Why don't you steer and leave the pushing to me?" said Fergus once they had got the van outside. Charlie nodded, more carefully this time, and got into the vehicle, winding down the window as he did so. That way he could continue talking to the footman and keep him in sight, too, framed as he was in the wing mirror. Physical exertion obviously put Fergus in the mood for conversation for they had only moved on a few yards before he was offering up more recollections of the recent past. "See, when Miss Fiona said my former job was waiting for me, it was a real lifeline. Our old man's house had been bombed, you see, and I didnae really have anywhere else to go." He paused for a moment before catching Charlie's eye in the mirror. "Sorry, I'm bending your ear, aren't I?" he added apologetically.

"*Listening is at least half of effective communication!*" said Charlie, mimicking the cadences of some hitherto forgotten army instructor. "At least, that's what they taught us during training," he added quickly, fearing the footman might think him pompous.

The footman evidently thought nothing of the kind. "Aye, well, good luck explaining that to Mr Ivan," he replied with a smile. "By the way, where do you want to park this thing?"

"I thought in front of the terrace, where the most people can hear."

"Good idea, radio man," said Fergus as he leant in to push some more.

Fiona ran up to the bandleader on the podium.

"Can you get them to stop playing for a while?" she asked whilst glancing at the other musicians. The bandleader nodded and directed the members of his band accordingly. Apart from oranges, the mood of mutual co-operation had been greatly aided by the surreptitious measures of whisky that had been distributed during the evening, and she soon had the attention of the gathering.

"Ladies and gentlemen," she began, "in a few moments an important announcement is going to be made and I'd like you all to hear it."

Lady Caird and Finlay exchanged surprised glances and everyone around them began to murmur in anticipation. Fiona then opened one of the French windows and, followed by Martha and Cameron, ran over to the balustrade.

"Is it time for the fireworks?" the little girl asked.

"Not just yet, sweetheart," said the Land Girl.

Peering into the darkness, she could just make out Charlie steering a van and Fergus pushing it. It was a lot easier for Charlie to see Fiona though, standing as she was with a blaze of light behind her. He leant out of the window and signalled she should now open all the other windows too. Fiona gave him a thumbs up to indicate she had understood but, as she glanced back inside the hall, she saw Ivan enter, evidently searching for her. Instead of going back indoors she directed Cameron and Martha to deputise whilst she ran around to the front of the castle, following the route Charlie had taken earlier.

"What's she doing?" Charlie asked the ghost as he watched through the windscreen.

The ghost, who was now in the passenger seat, merely shrugged and looked at his watch. "Ten minutes," was all he said in a flat monotone.

Back inside the great hall, search as he might, Ivan could see no trace of Fiona, but he did notice that everyone was looking expectantly towards the windows, which were being opened by the two children. Whatever this rabble were expecting, it wasn't him, and as he wasn't ready to make his announcement yet anyway, he went up the bandleader and gestured that he should start playing again. The bandleader sniffed the air at Ivan's approach, and it was only then that Ivan became aware of the haggis stuck to his hair and the collar of his jacket. With the music resumed, Ivan made a beeline for the cooler air of the terrace where there was no heat to accentuate the rich aroma of onion, spices, sheep's heart, liver and lungs that clung to him. He then pushed Martha and Cameron out of the way and slammed all the French windows shut again.

From his observation point, Charlie could also see Ivan out on the terrace. Deciding it might be a good idea to duck down, he then made frantic stop signals to Fergus by waving his arm through the open window. Fergus, grateful for the chance to stop pushing, adjusted the tarpaulin draped over the roof to aid concealment. Of course, the ghost, being invisible to all but Charlie, stayed exactly where he was, and Charlie, had he been less anxious, might safely have done the same.

For the fact was that Ivan was at a distinct disadvantage. Not only had he just left a brightly lit room and his eyes were still adjusting to the darkness but, like many stuck in a comfortable rut, he found it harder to spot what he wasn't looking for. It had been easy for him to notice empty shelves in the wine cellar because that's exactly what he had expected to find. On the other hand, the notion that a large mechanical beast might, at that very moment, be trundling through the undergrowth mere yards away, was quite inconceivable to him, therefore it remained invisible. Children, on the other hand, especially those with vivid imaginations, would have fared better. Which is a long way of explaining why the smarter adults in our story made sure they kept their youngsters on side. Ivan, blindly unaware of all this, ended up running around to the front of the castle instead.

Meanwhile, Fiona was already running up the stairs leading from the front entrance, which is where she intercepted Angus who had just emerged from the kitchen in red-eyed fury. He in turn was closely followed by Amy.

"Wait till I get my hands on that little runt," fumed the chef.

In the same instant Fiona realised that she could also hear music playing and she beckoned the other two to follow her back into the great hall.

"What did you start playing again for?" she asked the bandleader.

"The wee man told us to," the man replied, defensively.

Fiona followed the direction of his gaze and noticed that all the windows were closed again.

"I'll tell you when to start, okay?"

"Okay, okay," he replied. Wishing people would make up their minds, he directed the musicians to stop playing again.

Fiona then dragged Angus and Amy over to the windows. "Open them," she instructed, "open them all. After that, Angus you go help Fergus outside, and Amy, you stay here and make sure no one tries to block our shipping lanes."

Whilst Angus and Amy, with assistance from Martha and Cameron, obliged, Finlay came over to cross-examine Fiona.

"What's happened?"

"There's a *non*-something will," she answered hurriedly.

"Nuncupative," corrected the old man helpfully.

"That's it, only we're one witness short."

"Where there's a will there's a way."

"Do you really believe that?" she asked, her face betraying anxiety for the first time. Finlay smiled and held up two sets of crossed fingers and a moment later the girl had vanished into the night once more.

Leaning over the balcony she could see that the van was nearly in place, once it had flashed its lights, she returned to the open window and shouted to those gathered inside.

"If you'd all like to join me out here on the terrace."

At that moment Ivan re-entered the room and,

charging straight up to the bandleader, demanded, "What did you stop for? I didn't tell you to stop!"

The hapless bandleader, who was not by nature confrontational, merely inclined his head in the direction of Fiona. But by this time Ivan was in no mood to bandy words, either with her or anyone else. Instead he made a grab for the bandleader's megaphone.

"Here, give me that," he growled. The bandleader glanced at Fiona again and, seeing her shake her head, gamely attempted to wrestle it back. "I *said* give it to me!" Ivan persisted, now totally oblivious to all the eyes staring at him.

After his fingers had been prised off the voice horn one by one, the maestro let go.

"I may never wield the baton again," he wailed as he examined his mauled digits. But without the slightest sign of remorse, Ivan merely wiped the mouthpiece and lifted it to his face.

"Ladies and gentlemen," he began, "as I'm sure many of you are wondering what the future holds, I want to make a special announcement about the estate, and I can now tell you that…"

"What Ivan wants to say," interrupted Fiona from the other side of the room, "is that as 1946 is going to be such a special year for us…"

Her eyes darted around before settling on the fireplace. "And seeing how it will be the first full year of peace…" she continued as she ran over to the hearth and grabbed a piece of coal with some tongs, "we want you all to join in with an old New Year tradition. I've been reliably informed that it involves taking a piece of coal through the front door and out through the back for good luck. Will you help us do that?"

The loud cheers that greeted this suggestion brought a huge smile to her face for she knew they had effectively silenced Ivan, at least for the time being. "Splendid. Then follow me." Lifting the coal aloft and closely followed by Martha and Cameron, she led the guests out through the French windows in a long snaking procession.

Amy, who had positioned herself by their exit route, had a tray at the ready to collect any empty glasses from the passing throng. But, try as she might, it was a hit and miss operation – more miss than hit, as glass after glass hit the floor. But like a determined goalie, she reached to save every one, up, down, backwards, front and sideways. Ivan watched his audience diminish with obvious fury and the unfortunate bandleader was, once more, directly in the line of fire.

"Start playing, damn it!" ordered the little man. The bandleader did not understand this sudden change of mind and just looked at Ivan blankly.

"Go on, play, you imbecile," snarled Ivan.

"How does that one go again?" asked the bandleader, retreating behind a music stand.

If looks could kill, the maestro would've have joined Glenn Miller on the great bandstand in the sky at that moment. However, before you could say *Moonlight Serenade*, the lead musician took the initiative and started his colleagues off again. They were playing music, but not as we know it, for with their conductor still seriously distracted by Ivan, the tempo was wildly erratic.

As she was leading the guests along the terrace, Fiona

glanced at Charlie who was giving her desperate *five-minute* signals. She nodded to show she understood the time constraint before accelerating her pace round to the front of the house.

Inside the van, the ghost was staring at his watch and looking even more morose.

"It's actually zero hour minus four minutes and forty-five seconds."

"Sorry," replied Charlie, tension clearly detectable in his voice.

"Stop apologising and check your equipment."

The radio repairman nodded and switched on the speaker, which crackled with static.

This was a signal to Fergus. Cupping his hands together he made the sound of an owl and the scruffy boys emerged from the bushes to assist him in removing the tarpaulin. It was expertly done and seconds later the footman appeared at the window gathering the sheet up under his arm. "If you two are all set, we'll get to our battle stations."

Charlie nodded and Fergus and his nephews departed at the double.

"How's the head?" asked the ghost.

"Still a bit groggy," replied Charlie, touched by the note of concern. He turned to study the face of his passenger just in case there was a smirk there.

Seeing none, he continued quietly, "Just don't leave your name until the end this time, all right? Otherwise we might be right back where we started. Oh, and don't say house when you mean castle. It's not just any old castle either, it's Castle Caird – the castle that cared."

"And why don't you stop nit-picking and just repeat

everything I say?" grumbled the ghost, back to his impatient self again. Earlier in the day Charlie might have taken offence, that is the old, thin-skinned Charlie would have taken offence, but now he understood that Caird was nervous and trying to cover it up. They were both nervous of course but, crucially, the repairman now knew he was not nervous alone.

"Echo by name, echo by nature, that's me," he sighed philosophically. Leaning forward he reached into the glove compartment and removed a tin of boiled sweets. After offering one to his companion he took one himself.

"Soldier Charles and Citizen Charlie – together we'll get the job done," ruminated the ghost as he sucked the lozenge.

"Is that the answer to the riddle of the complete man?" Charlie asked.

The ghost turned to face him. "All I've learned from this war is that you don't have to be good to be brave, but you do have to be brave to be good. And that's not just the good man you are, Charlie, but the better, more fulfilled and compassionate people we all have it in ourselves to be, given half a chance."

"Or the ghost of one," smiled Charlie.

"Yes," Caird almost smiled back. "And maybe that's all that peace really is."

Chapter Twenty-One

A SHOUT THAT WAS RECOGNISABLY FIONA'S WAS audible through the open window.

"Back onto the terrace, everybody," it announced. Looking up they saw a surging mass of people starting to gather and, in their midst, the Land Girl was leaning over the balustrade and giving Charlie the thumbs-up signal again. Charlie took a deep breath, returned her signal and picked up the microphone.

Up above and concealed from their view, Ivan pushed past Lady Caird and Finlay.

"Come inside everybody. Come inside, there's no point in standing out here in the cold."

"But you'll get a much better view of the fireworks if you stay where you are," countered Fiona.

Charles looked at Charlie. "Ready?" he asked.

Charlie nodded.

"I, Charles James Caird, have entrusted Charles Goodman with the solemn task of relaying my last will and testament to those gathered here."

Then it was Charlie's turn, "I, Charles James Caird

have entrusted Charles Goodman with the solemn task of relaying my last will and testament to those gathered here."

"And it is my express wish that my beloved fiancé, Fiona Maclean, maintains her stewardship of the estate."

"And it is my express wish that my beloved fiancé, Fiona maintain, er, Maclean the stewardship, er, that Fiona Maclean maintains the stewardship of the estate."

Charlie coughed and wiped away the beads of sweat that had already started to form on his brow.

Up on the terrace Finlay took advantage of the brief pause to catch up, as he was transcribing everything he heard into a pocket notebook. The whistles and cheers of those gathered around him were making it difficult and he strained to catch what came next.

Inside the van the ghost was pressing on. "And that my mother, my fiancé and her descendants remain in the domestic quarters of Castle Caird…"

"And that my mother, my fiancé and her descendants remain in the domestic quarters of Castle Caird…" repeated Charlie.

"For as long as they all so wish."

"For as long as they all so wish," echoed the radio repairman.

On hearing this, Fiona gave Lady Caird an enormous hug but Ivan, who was close by, had already heard far too much for his liking.

"I will not be denied any longer," he muttered grinding one fist into the other. "I will not, *will not*."

"No," said Lady Caird, shooting out a restraining arm, "*what you will not do* is disregard the final wishes of my son!"

But he had no more intention of listening to her than to anyone else. The idea of entitlement had rooted itself so firmly in his mind that it blocked out all other considerations. A lifetime of imagined slights, seemingly the inevitable consequence of being the poor relation, was now about to be redressed. So, pushing the old lady's arm aside, he went and vaulted straight over the balustrade! And, even though the drop was longer than expected, he was possessed by the kind of manic energy that overrides any normal sense of pain. Scrambling up again, he was beside the van in no time at all. Watching from above, Amy put down her tray and went back indoors.

Once beside the van, Ivan tried to pull the driver's door open, but it was being firmly held from the inside. Pounding on the window, which by then had also been closed, only seemed to enrage him further. "Why don't you take your third-rate magic tricks and that tatty costume and, and…" Charlie, microphone still in hand, had thrown himself across the ghost in order to prevent Ivan from getting in through the passenger door, and it was while he was sprawled in this way that the ghost decided to continue.

"And furthermore, that the remainder of the buildings be given over to the army for use as a convalescent home by its personnel, *all* ranks of its personnel."

At this Charlie couldn't help looking up at the ghost in surprised approval.

"And furthermore, that the remainder of the buildings be given over to the army, for use as a convalescent home by all ranks of its personnel."

By this time Amy had returned to the terrace handing Lady Caird a fishing rod and line. Although initially puzzled by the presentation, the old lady soon cottoned on thanks to the housekeeper's pointing and miming. Meanwhile, Ivan had climbed onto the hood of the vehicle and from there onto its roof. Once positioned there he tried to wrestle the speaker free whilst Charlie's voice continued to boom from inside it.

"… as a place of peace and tranquillity where they can recuperate before returning to civilian life."

By this time Fiona had also arrived, but her decision to take the steps rather than the balustrade had given Ivan time to claim the high ground. All she could do now was try to grab his ankles. But no sooner had she done so than he kicked her off, causing her fall to the ground and into the beam of approaching headlights.

As Fiona was tumbling, Lady Caird was casting and, much to her delight, she soon hooked her line onto the vent of Ivan's jacket. Though a fishing line pitted against the strength of a grown man may not seem a terribly even match, Ivan's position just then was a lot more precarious than he would have liked. Having run across the grass, his shoes had been slippery when he first climbed up, and now that he had been moving around up there, the roof was like an ice rink. The dazzle from the headlights put him at a further disadvantage. He heard the sound of brakes and an engine stopping, but the lights remained fixed upon him. Two people emerged from the glare, both hurrying. One, a woman in a headscarf, went straight to Fiona, the other, a man, was coming towards him.

"Detective Constable Saunders, what exactly is going on here?"

"Arrest this man," ordered Ivan as he stamped on the

roof below and nearly lost his balance again, "he's making a disturbance."

"It rather seems as though you're the one that's doing that, sir," said Saunders noticing the line that was continually tugging at Ivan's coat. "And that you've been caught in the act too."

At the other end of the line Lady Caird was using all her strength to reel in her catch whilst Amy provided extra leverage by wrapping her arms around the older woman's waist. Behind her the scruffy boys plus Martha and Cameron followed suit, arranging themselves in descending order of height like a well-drilled circus troupe.

Ivan tried to remove his jacket with one arm whilst clinging onto the speaker with the other.

"Not me, you idiot, him!" he said stamping the roof for emphasis. But with fifty per cent of his gripping power now gone, it only took one final tug of the line for him to slide off and end up face to face with the copper, a copper who wasn't taking any flannel.

"Besides insulting a police officer, you do realise you shouldn't interrupt the reading of a will?"

"What you just heard wasn't a will, it was the ravings of a lunatic."

"It sounded like a will to me," Saunders said evenly.

"The man's quite mad," Ivan protested.

By now all the McPherson children were leaning on the balustrade whilst Marge's brood had emerged from the car and assembled around their mother.

"What do you say to that, children?" asked Saunders, looking round and providing the age-old prompt line."

"Oh no he isn't!" came the unanimous reply.

"The balcony and the stalls say not," said Saunders with a slight smile.

"Don't forget the physical violence and the wilful damage to a family heirloom," Marge called out as she helped Fiona to her feet.

"That as well, thank you. That's quite a list we're compiling here," noted the copper before snapping a handcuff around one of Ivan's wrists.

"I'll report you for this," Ivan exploded.

"Your word against that of all these people? Save it for the magistrate. He'll give you the one thing you seem unable to give anyone else – a hearing."

The sight of the handcuffs was a signal to the onlookers to draw closer and there was a general movement down the steps. Although Ivan searched their faces, he couldn't find a sympathetic one amongst them.

"It's a conspiracy," spluttered the prisoner.

"No," Saunders replied sternly, "it's a consensus."

As he bundled his charge past the van, Charlie got out and held out his notebook. "I think you might be wanting this, Sid!" It wasn't much of a speech but it spoke volumes to his former comrade.

"You all right, mate?" the copper enquired doubling back and using his free hand, first to take the book and then to shake the hand of his friend.

"Do you two know each other?" asked Fiona, now fully recovered from her fall.

"I had the honour of serving with this splendid chap in France," answered the policeman proudly.

"Seems like you've found your second witness after all," Finlay whispered in the Land Girl's ear before turning to the newly reunited pals. "But if I could just get you gentlemen to sign my transcription. Oh, and anything relevant in your own little book there," he continued, proffering a pen.

Charlie glanced at Fiona, unsure as to the old man's identity, but seeing her nod enthusiastically, he did as requested before passing his pen on to Saunders.

"But how did you know where I'd gone?" he asked while his friend was writing.

"After you took off, your sister and I put two and two together."

"And got six in an Austin 7!" added Marge, with a smile.

"Oh Margie!" cried Charlie, "I forgot to close the door to the shed, didn't I?"

"That's all right, love," she replied in her most sisterly tone, "Sergeant Saunders explained you had an important business errand to run. But maybe I should get one of those weighted things so it'll shut all by itself in future."

Up on the balcony, the same hearty guest who had been so enthusiastic about shooting at saucers that morning announced, "Thirty seconds till the chimes," and immediately a murmur of excitement rose amongst the crowd.

"Did Charles say anything else before he – died?" asked Fiona.

"They were all pretty far gone by the time we reached them," Saunders replied gently.

"Charlie here had tried to send a warning, but when they turned back they walked straight into enemy fire at close range."

The Land Girl took a deep breath.

"Fifteen," shouted the hearty guest.

"But just as I was taking down his name," Charlie began in a faraway voice, "there was this bellowing sound, and for a moment I thought it was coming from him…"

"Oh, no," interrupted Fiona, unable to stop herself.

"It wasn't, though," Charlie continued.

1944

Charlie was bent low beside the recumbent figure of Charles Caird but looked up from his notebook long enough to notice a stray cow that had appeared in the lane up ahead. He paid the animal scant attention and returned his focus to the dying man who was muttering something.

"The land is mine?" the radio man repeated and was just about to write it down when, with a supreme effort, Caird shook his head.

The cow, which had evidently been badly spooked by the recent sound of gunfire, was now trotting backwards and forwards, trying to decide which way to run next and Saunders' gaze kept darting between the animal and the tragic tableau beside him. "The lane is mined!" Caird finally managed to croak and at that moment the cow suddenly started to charge straight towards them. Saunders grabbed Charlie and pulled him into a ditch where, a split second later, they were showered with the debris of a large explosion, one of the pieces gashing Charlie across the forehead during its trajectory.

*

"Ten!" announced the hearty guest.

"Nine, eight…" other voices began to shout, but Charlie barely noticed.

"He was saving our lives," he said to Fiona, moved by the fresh recollection.

"Look around, he still is," she answered softly.

Charlie turned to look at the passenger seat, but the ghost had gone. Only a crumpled sweet wrapper remained on the leather.

And then the clock struck twelve, followed by loud cheers of "Happy New Year" from the terrace. A few moments after that *Auld Lang Syne* was ringing off the stonework. Charlie looked up and addressed the air. "Did I decipher that correctly, soldier?"

"If you can't see him anymore, then you must have done," replied the Land Girl.

"Freed into the ether," said the radio repairman, before climbing onto the running board to check the speaker for damage.

"Everything okay up there?" Fiona asked as he tested the bolts.

"Me or it?"

"Both."

"Oh aye, we're sound enough, I reckon," he said stepping down again.

Just then there was a loud bang as the first firework burst overhead. Charlie cowered slightly before pulling himself up to his full height. He looked at the happy faces that surrounded him and then up at the multicoloured spectacle above. "But I'm staying tuned," he smiled.

Bibliography

Aldgate, Anthony and Richards, Jeffrey, *Britain Can Take It*, Edinburgh University Press, 1994

Alexander, Larry, *Biggest Brother – The Life of Major Dick Winters, The Man Who Led the Band of Brothers*, Nal Caliber, 2006

Baron, Alexander, *From the City, From the Plough*, IWM, 2019

Calder, Angus, *The People's War*, Random House, 1992

Christie, Ian, *Powell, Pressburger and Others*, British Film Institute, 1978

Deeping, Warwick, *Laughing House*, Cassel and Company Ltd, 1946

Gillies, Midge, *The Barbed Wire University*, Aurum Press, 2012

Goulston, Mark, *Post Traumatic Stress Syndrome for Dummies*, Wiley Publishing, 2008

Harper, Sue, *Gainsborough Melodrama*, British Film Institute, 1983

Hillary, Richard, *The Last Enemy*, Macmillan, 1942

Kershaw, Alex, *Jack London – A Life*, Flamingo, 1998

Linklater, Eric, *Private Angelo*, Jonathan Cape, 1946

Noble, Christina, *Ardkinglas – The Biography of a Highland Estate*, Berlinn Ltd, 2018

Sackville-West, Vita, *The Women's Land Army*, Michael Joseph, 1944

Stockdale, Jim, *Thoughts of a Philosophical Fighter Pilot*, Hoover Institution Press, 1995

Sullivan, Jill Alexander, *The Politics of the Pantomime: Regional Identity in the Theatre*, University of Hertfordshire, 2011

Millie Taylor, *British Pantomime Performance*, Intellect Books, 2007

Additional Sources

The Tom Harrison Mass Observation Archive housed at Sussex University. Town and Country Surveys, Boxes 11, 19 and 20.

Acknowledgements

J UST AS CHARLIE WAS THE ONLY PERSON ABLE TO
see the ghost of Charles Caird, I am the only person
who can acknowledge all the help I received whilst
working on this piece of writing. Like a ghost, it is also
something that has "shape-shifted" from one form into
another. In the first instance, *Charlie Echo* was conceived
as a screenplay, and I have to say some of the most unjustly
invisible people around are the legions of story editors
and consultants who work behind the scenes on script
development. It's therefore great to have an opportunity to
"put some names out there." All of these generous, smart
people took the time to read early drafts, make helpful
comments and ask the searching questions that helped me
say what I wanted to say.

Appropriately enough, I had my first meeting with
Kate Leys whilst attending a writing workshop in a Scottish
castle in 2011, and several more face-to-face meetings
followed later in London. My debt to Olivia Stewart is even
greater, for not only did she chat to me from her home in
Rome, providing splendid notes and suggestions along the

way, but she also, along with Charles Rees, gave me my first professional film cutting room job back in 1994. The final member of this trio is Karol Griffiths, whom I must thank for her wisdom in sending me back to Dickens, the father of all modern Christmas stories.

Reaching further back still, it was historian, writer and lecturer Sue Harper, whose name also features in the bibliography, who first encouraged me to visit the Mass Observation Archive held at Sussex University. At the time she was supervising tutor for my undergraduate thesis at Portsmouth Polytechnic and, as well as teaching me the rudiments of research and writing, she opened my eyes to the treasure trove founded by anthropologist Tom Harrison, poet Charles Madge and film-maker Humphrey Jennings. The excitement of going through some of the transcribed conversations held there has stayed with me ever since.

Producer Pip Piper had the insight to get me to reverse-engineer and "work back from the pitch". He also encouraged me to road-test the story by running it past some of his students on the MA Film Marketing Course at Birmingham City University. So my thanks also go to Anthony Evans, Kara Hanna, Corina Osei and Yu Ida Wang.

Pantomimes should be for all ages, but it wasn't until I had the chance to sit down with producer Daniel Konrad Cooper that I felt ready to let Margie's brood and all the MacPherson children take their rightful places. Thanks, Dan!

The "magic dust" came courtesy of David Wood, justifiably dubbed National Children's Dramatist, who generously provided the blurb for the cover, Helen Wiltshire at Warner Chappell UK, who made it possible for Charles and Charlie to duet like "Old Cowhands", and the amazingly helpful James Peak who, in turn, put me in touch with Julie O'Doherty, the perfect proofreader. Further afield, and proving Marconi's theory still holds good, more invisible assistance came from Thelma Schoonmaker who, despite being incredibly busy, was still willing to "put in a word for me" from the other side of the Atlantic.

Then there's Mr Lee Ingleby!

It was Lee who truly gave the characters their voice and his tour de force reading of the audio book was a writer's dream that also fed back into the manuscript.

Last, but by no means least, I must thank my former Imperial War Museum colleagues Peter Hallinan, for his knack with titles, and David Finch for spotting relevant film footage and introducing me to members of the Duxford Radio Society. And, as books are judged by their covers, further acknowledgements must go to Ben Knock for allowing me to snap away at his excellent Military Wireless Museum in Kidderminster and Messrs Harry and Gerald Prime of Frontline Figures for granting permission to feature a pair of their hand-painted metal soldiers.

Take a bow, everyone.

Matador